OUR TYPE OF LOVE

CHELSEA MARIA

MY LETTER TO YOU!

Hey Loves,

Thank you for all your support and continuing this journey with me. I wasn't sure if I wanted to give a warning about the emotional topics discussed in this book. If you are familiar with my work thus far, then you know I embrace the challenge of writing emotional stories. Our Type of Love is an emotional story that deals with miscarriages and infertility. As both of those topics can be sensitive triggers for those who have or are experiencing them, I pray you find comfort and enjoy Kellon and Delilah's story.

XOXO,

Chelsea Maria

PROLOGUE

K ellon

"KC, we're pulling up. You got less than ten minutes to get out of there." Khiver's voice boomed through the phone.

Running a trembling hand over my head, I sighed. "Is…is she with you?" My chest constricted as I sat waiting. No air filled my lungs. I couldn't breathe.

"Um, w-we, she…I don't know where she is, Kellon. That's why I need you out of there. You and I both know she can't find you before we do. I'll call you back when I'm downstairs." Without another word, my brother disconnected the call. I know he wanted to say more. I could hear the disappointment in his voice.

I fucked up.

Bad.

The body lying next to me awakening snapped me out of the depressed state I placed myself in. "Babe, why are you up so early? Is it time for you to go?" The feel of her hand touching my back felt like a cast iron branding my skin causing me to jump up.

"Kellon, what's the matter?" Chuckling in annoyance, I ignored the innocence in her voice. She and I both knew what was wrong. We crossed a line that shouldn't have ever been crossed.

Standing over the bed, I ran a hand over my head as I stared down at the soft brown leg that freed itself from the tangle of the sheets. I knew what lay behind those covers that clung to curves my hands had become familiar with during the night. There was no denying the beauty in her face, and from the smirk on her lips, she knew it too. Though she was beautiful, she wasn't my Delilah, and I gave her a piece of me that didn't belong to her.

Sitting up, she let the sheet puddle around her waist giving me one last view of her succulent breasts. "Will you call me? I can meet you whenever she isn't around?" I quickly snapped out of the lustful haze her body put me in and begged my legs not to give out on me.

I felt weak. Physically, mentally, and emotionally.

Delilah.

Immediately, the guilt plagued me. Heart first. Shoving my hands in the pockets of my jeans, the pain of my betrayal dug deeper as my right hand touched the velvet box. My throat burned as a massive amount of emotions hit me all at once. I've never been a man who expressed his emotions or was emotionally led, but then Delilah entered my world and shook it up for the better.

She taught me that it was okay to feel. It was okay to be loved and to love. She showed that what my parents and grandparents had, real love, was obtainable with her.

Staring into the eyes of the woman lying in the hotel bed I saw red. Not because of the predicament we were in, or because I fell for her luscious charm. I saw red because all I could imagine was Delilah doing the same to me. God have mercy on the man's soul because he was a dead man.

If she ever found out about my one time of dishonesty, she'd leave me. My world couldn't leave me, and I prayed God showed me mercy one last time and kept this between the three of us.

A knock came from the door letting me know Khiver had arrived.

"Be easy," I said as I admired her beauty one last time. My steps to the door were heavy. The guilt of it all weighed me down. I had to get myself together before I faced Delilah. She knew me better than anyone and could read me like a book. This secret wasn't one she could ever find out. I couldn't lose my world over one mistake.

KELLON

N ine Years Later

I n the twelve years that I've graced the stage and sold out stadium after stadium, nothing felt better than standing in the middle of the stage holding out the mic while thousands of fans rapped along to my lyrics. They paid to see me perform but it felt like I was the one getting the show. People danced. Swayed and bopped to the beat. From the distance that I could see, some wore shirts with my name plastered across their chest. Some had signs that expressed their love for me. In all, no matter how many times I sold out, each concert felt like my first.

I named the tour The Closed Chapters Tour for a reason. Not only was this my last tour of the year but my run with Gump Records had come to an end. The question of me resigning with the label after the tour had been plaguing my mind for months. I knew the direction I wanted to head in with my music, but I also knew the politics of the music industry.

Since the beginning of my rap career, I've held this sense of pride for not conforming and setting myself apart from the rest. My lyrics weren't about material things or degrading women. I rapped about real life issues and struggles. Lyrics that uplifted kids, men, and women to be more than the enigma society has set. Fans connected with me because I told their stories. I kept it real, and people respected me for that. Now, I wanted to rap on a deeper level, and I hoped these same fans that filled this arena would still rock with me once my new single dropped next week.

As DJ Skew switched gears and changed the beat to my latest release, my eyes drifted to the middle of the arena near the engineering section. Standing up on the man-made platform stood my world dressed in samples from my upcoming clothing line, Redemption.

Like the others among her, she bopped her head and snapped her fingers ready for me to rap. Her smile grew when she took notice that I was watching her. It didn't matter if a million people swarmed around her, I'd still be able to spot my world without hesitation.

"Miami, this is my last show of the tour. I had to end it at home. Man, the energy in here is insane." Hopping onto the stacked speakers, I threw up my 'L's.' "Y'all ready to turn up one last time with me?" The screams vibrated off the stage as I jumped down. "DJ Skew, let's go." The screams grew louder and louder. My heart pumped as the adrenaline raced through my veins.

To anyone else, it looked like I was pointing just to point at something random in the crowd. No. This song was meant for somebody in particular. Someone special. I wanted to make sure she knew that. "My little mama, this is for you," I spoke in the mic. The fans went wild. They knew who this song was for.

As it had done a million times before, her face lit up as she jumped up and down when I began rapping the words to 'You're just my type.' I wrote the song two hours after I laid eyes on her nine years ago in college. Delilah Cambridge was my world. My everything.

The U.S. and European tour drained me dry. Traveling nonstop took a heavy toll on my body. People saw the airplanes and different locations and thought I was living the life. Don't get me wrong, I'm blessed that my job requires me to travel, but most of the time I rarely get to enjoy it. Either I'm performing, recording, or being interviewed.

The downside to being on the go so much was the exertion. Tired was an understatement at this point. All I wanted to do was go home and sleep in my bed. I hadn't seen the inside of my house in over six months. The only reason I knew I still owned it and squatters hadn't taken over was because my parents checked on it while I was on the road.

An hour later I thanked the crowd and instructed security to get my wife. By the time she made it to me, all the VIP fans had received everything included in their package including a picture with me, an autograph, and samples from my clothing line.

"Excuse me, can I have your autograph?" Hearing her voice lulled me into a relaxed mood.

Right away my security escorted everyone out my dressing room. They knew what time it was when Lilah came in. My attention was hers and no else.

"It all depends. Are you sure you're a fan of mine?" Licking my lips, I took in her appearance. Delilah could wear dirty rags, and she'd still be the most beautiful woman to me. Reaching out, I grabbed her wrist and pulled her into my chest. A hard day of work felt worth it whenever I looked down into those brandy eyes and watching her plump red stained lips curve into a smile.

Her eyes watched my lips. Reading what I was saying instead of listening with her ears. Wrapping a hand behind her neck, I pecked her lips. "I missed you." Running my nose along her jaw, I distracted her to turn her hearing aid on. "Stop reading my lips."

"I forgot to turn it back on once we got backstage. I thought I could keep it on during your performance, but your fans were on another level tonight. How do you feel?" Seeing the affection glowing in her eyes caused me to smile.

Her eyes were the tunnels to her heart and each time I took that journey to look into the depths of her love I got sucked in. I found myself undeniably smitten. When it came to the woman in my arms, I unapologetically showcased my love.

"Good. Tonight was amazing. Are you going to the club with me? I have to make an appearance, but that's it." I bit the corner of my lip as I waited for her to answer me.

No matter the number of years that passed I never got enough of being around my wife. I genuinely liked being around her. Before anything else, she and I were friends and then lovers. Having her travel with me was nonnegotiable. In the nine years that she and I have been together, I can count on one hand the number of shows she has missed. Each tour I have gone on she has been present. Interviews, music videos, and appearances have all been done with her standing in her place. At my side.

"Depends on where you're going. If it's KOD or The Office, I'm not going. I've seen enough strippers to last me a lifetime." She playfully pulled on my beard.

The mention of strippers caused my eyes to take in her appearance. Delilah Mari was beautiful. Ebony skin that made me drool no matter the time or place. Her self-care routine caused me to groan on many nights, mainly when I wanted to cuddle up. Lilah went by order and my antsy behavior didn't put a wrench into her regimen. It didn't work like that. After her showers, she or I, mostly me, rubbed her soft skin down in a natural body butter or oils that made her smell intoxicating.

Then those eyes, the color of the most expensive brandy. I could stare at her all day if she let me. There was no such thing as an intense moment. Like my body needed water and food to function, my soul feeds off that palpable energy shared when our eyes connected.

When we spoke of children, I prayed God spared me if he blessed me with a daughter. My heart couldn't take it if she grew up to be shaped like her mother. My gun collection wasn't that big, and there weren't enough bullets in the world to keep these no-good dudes away.

Magnificent. That's the parental advisory word I used when describing her body that I thanked her ancestors for daily. Out of all her features and body measurements, her cute little button nose and baby doll eyes were my favorite feature.

On the night of my shows, she wore a piece from my clothing line to build the hype. She'd post a picture on her social media accounts and next thing you know, her DM's were flooded with people wanting to purchase her outfit.

Tonight, she wore the black and red t-shirt dress with my logo plastered along the sides. The fishnet stockings and combat heeled boots made it look edgy and sexy. The shirt covered enough but I made a mental note to tell my designer to lengthen the pieces he created specifically for my wife.

"It's at Live. You don't have to change. Khiver said we could head there right after we leave." I reached for my phone and texted my security to let them know that we were headed out.

"Okay, cool. Let's go." She grabbed her purse just as the security came in.

When I first started out rapping, I wasn't clean and had a heavy hand in the streets. I performed at night and ran the streets during the day alongside my brother and Father. Along the way I acquired enemies. Even though a decade had passed since I was in the game, there was always one or two fools that would come lurking around out of the blue and thought I became a square because I got my money legally and would try me. I played no games especially when it came to the safety of those around me.

I watched Diego and Bruce escort my wife out and head in the direction of the tunnel that led to the underground parking garage. Tyson and X escorted me out the back entrance. When I was on tour or performing, we always arrived and left separate. We road on the same tour bus and flew together, but when it came to anything else, we were separate. It took one bullet to bust a window for me to realize that people were vicious, and bullets didn't have names.

"Boss, Diego said they are out back. Khiver said to bring you through the front. What you want to do?" X informed me.

The blackout tint of the vehicle hid my scrutinizing eyes. Clubs made me uneasy. There were too many people confined to a small space that made it difficult to flee if need be. Regardless of this being my hometown or not, this was still Miami. "Has security reached inside yet?" I took in the line and sighed. Maybe I should've had Delilah go home.

"Yes, sir. All floors have been secured."

When Delilah accompanied me to club appearances, we followed the same rules. I went in first to scope out the scene, and then security would bring her through the back entrance. Sending a text to make sure she was good, I checked my waist one last time. Once she responded that she was waiting on me, I got out. "Let's go."

"I love you, KC."

"Marry me, KC."

Although I remained humble about my success, it still felt good to hear the screams of my fans. I waved and gave my signature smile before heading into the club. Immediately my eyes searched through the crowd, eyeing the exit signs and scoping out the scene. Walking to the VIP section, I navigated between nodding to people who spoke to me and making out the security. A few blended in with the crowd while the others were standing tall and broad.

The owner of the club gave us the top-level VIP area that was off in the cut but provided an excellent view to see the entire floor. A see-through red tinted glass wrapped around the area. It offered a sound barrier that decreased the music and noise from the main level.

Wasn't long before the champagne girls brought bottles and my team spread out. Surveying the club one last time, I relaxed and texted by brother Khiver to bring me Delilah. Out of the corner of my eye, I watched Bruce walk in first with Delilah sandwiched between him and Bruce. "Mama, what you want to drink?" I asked as she sat on my lap.

"Amaretto sour please." Her drink choice didn't surprise me. It was her signature drink.

"How long you want to stay?" Khiver asked as he poured himself a glass of Patron.

Tapping Lilah on the butt, I nodded for her to answer my brother. "I'm feeling the vibe and music. At least an hour. Is that good for you, babe?" She turned to look at me.

"You heard the boss."

Khiver nodded, "Cool. I'm going to talk to the owner."

"Delilah Mari," I spoke directly in her ear. Even though the music up here was a lot lower than the main floor, the way her hearing aid worked, it lowered background noise and amplified voices, making her ears extra sensitive.

"Yes, Kellon." She batted her eyes while sipping from her glass. For a moment, my gaze was stuck on the way she wrapped her lips around the straw and teased it with her tongue.

Smirking, I ran a hand over her thigh. "You slipping on your job, Mama."

The gasp that came out of her mouth caused me to chuckle. Placing a hand over her chest, her eyes ballooned. "Me? Slipping? How have I slipped from my duties?" Her dramatics caused me to smile.

"I ain't felt them lips since earlier. I don't like that. You need to fix that before I fix it for you." Seeing her brandy eyes lower instantly and fill with desire sent a chill down my spine. Everything about Delilah Mari intrigued me. Second by second. Minute by minute. She fascinated and captivated me at first glance.

Wrapping her arms around my neck, she pulled me closer to her. "I'm sorry, baby. You forgive me?"

Before I could answer, she captured my lips with hers. Whenever we kissed, we created the perfect ballad. Each time her tongue slow danced with mine, the harmony of our love seeped into the air creating an atmosphere of euphoria.

No one could tell me that our love for each other could dry out. Our love didn't run dry because each time we kissed we re-watered the root.

DELILAH

"**Y**ou are so precious," I whispered as I rocked back and forth holding little Jace. He entered the world less than forty-eight hours ago, and already he captured my heart.

"He's so quiet with you. When I hold him all he does is cry." Hearing Nikki's voice crack broke my heart. Like most new moms, she had a hard time adjusting. She hoped that Jace would sleep during the night while her husband worked, and during the day they'd bond while he laid quietly in her arms. Little Jace had other plans that included exercising his infant lungs all times of the day. He operated off his own schedule.

Standing, with quiet steps, I walked over and handed little Jace to his mother. "Nikki, we talked about this. Babies can sense when you are nervous or scared. Would you not cry if you knew that the person holding you were afraid they would drop or smother you? Breathe and relax. The hard part is over. You made it full term and delivered a healthy baby. You did that. Now, the fun begins. Enjoy being a mother."

"Thank you so much, Delilah. I see why you are known as the baby whisperer." She giggled as she prepared to nurse Jace.

It wasn't my first time seeing a baby nurse from their mother's breast, and it wouldn't be the last. The sting in my chest created this illusion of longing. No matter how much I tried to leave my personal issues outside the hospital, I couldn't. Each time a baby was placed in my arms, I became emotionless to my reality which in return created zaps of pain.

"You ever thought of becoming a midwife? The gift you have shouldn't be confined to rocking babies for a few hours a day." Nikki asked as she smiled down at Jace.

Feeling the shift in my mood, I shrugged with a smile, and I gathered my things. "I have. Maybe one day. Remember what I said, enjoy and relax. I'll be back tomorrow." I kissed Jace on the cheek and walked out.

I felt closed in and began to feel sweat form across my brow as I shifted from one foot to the other waiting for the elevator to reach the ground floor. The minute the doors opened I sprinted out and jogged to my car. Gripping my steering wheel, I begged myself to cry. Tears cleansed the soul, and right now I needed my soul cleansed.

Nothing happened, but the sting in my chest grew until it reached the pit of my gut. Those closest to me called me a fool who liked self-inflicted pain because I placed myself in the line of fire each time I stepped foot inside the hospital. I didn't see it that way. In a sense, that place held the cure to what was causing my heart to break.

The blaring of my phone caused me to jump. Taking out my phone, I sighed heavily at my husband's handsome face on the screen. Even in this moment of self-pity, I found myself biting down hard on my bottom lip to block the smile that wanted to surface. He and I were in sync like that. Able to feel the others mood and emotional changes.

Miles away from one another and our hearts still communicated like two walkie-talkies. As much as I enjoyed hearing his voice serenade in my ear, I wasn't in the mood. Instead, I texted my best friend Woody and asked her to meet me for drinks.

It took me less than thirty minutes to make it to Shooters in down-town Las Olas. Usually, I went home and stripped out of my scrubs, but today I didn't care that the hospital musk clung to me.

"Hey, boo." Woody stood from the bar stool and hugged me.

"Hey, friend." I held her tight and felt a little joy when my eyes misted. "I love your hugs, Woody." Releasing her, I took a seat next to her.

Willamina "Woody" August and I have been friends since our sophomore year in high school. She's the sister that I always wanted. I called her my chocolate angel because, without her, I'd be a total and complete mess. She comforted me when my parents died and never complained when I clung to her after the passing of my Grandmother.

"Tell me why you're still in scrubs. You never come out in the hospital gear. I can see the stains from baby puke." She wagged a finger over a puke spot and turned up her nose.

I giggled before signaling for the waiter. After placing my drink order, I turned my attention towards her. "I couldn't go home. Kellon would only bombard me with endless questions, and I didn't feel like answering him."

"I don't get it, Lilah. You work at that place like it is going to heal you. Why do you self-inflict pain on yourself?" See what I mean? Everyone around me thought I was playing a dangerous game of Russian Roulette that would eventually leave me strapped in an asylum.

The truth is, I didn't know the answer to that question. No matter how many times I told myself I would quit as a baby rocker, the minute I stepped foot on the baby nursey floor every thought of stopping went out the window.

"Woody, it's not those babies fault that I can't carry a child. In a weird twisted way, they bring me peace." I cringed at my own words.

She wrapped her arm around my shoulders and kissed my temple. "I'm sorry, Lilah. I just feel like it's torture to work there that's all. What does Kellon think?"

A fermented taste coated my tongue. My eyes flooded with tears at the mention of my husband and his feelings on the matter of me not being able to carry his children. Lord knows I tried. Three times, and each time I'm left more and more soulless.

"He... he is supportive as he always is. We've been married for seven years, Woody. Seven years. In the beginning, I cared nothing about getting pregnant. It was the height of his career, and we were constantly on the road. No way did I want to bring a baby into that. Now, when I want a child, God keeps opening my womb only to slam the door when I get to a certain point." Exhaling, I took a deep breath. "Sometimes I feel like I'm useless. Inadequate. I'm a woman who can't have children."

For a moment neither of us said anything. Part of me wanted to apologize for what I said because I knew Woody and her husband Carter were in the process of trying for a baby. At no point did I want her to feel like I was talking about her because I wasn't. I was talking about my own broken womb.

"I'm sorry, Woody. That wasn't geared towards you but myself." I squeezed her hand as she smiled.

"I know you meant no harm. Can we change the subject to something fun like our girl's trip coming up soon?" Woody started dancing in her seat.

I clapped my hands in excitement. I needed a break and these next couple of weeks couldn't come fast enough. "Yes, about this trip. We are going to have a ball. I planned so many activities." I did what I did best, shove my feelings under the rug and pretend that they weren't there. Pretended that the pain no longer stung. Pretended that I was okay.

In the last five years, I've suffered three miscarriages. The first two ended at ten weeks. This last one went well into the second trimester. Kellon and I felt like we were finally going to have our family expanded. The baby bump sprouted, and we even went so far as to start decorating the nursery. At our next appointment, we were going to find out the sex of the baby, and I had already begun the preparations for a gender reveal party.

One day, in the shower, the water going down the drain turned crimson. Before the first surge of pain hit I already knew what was happening. At that point, I had become a pro at losing my babies.

I wanted a child with every fiber of my being. I wanted to give my husband a child.

Instead of hardening my heart towards the misfortune, I continued to volunteer at Jackson Hospital as a baby rocker. I continued to hug and love on those babies that needed my attention the most. I allowed my pain and suffering to be a comfort blanket for the motherless infant.

To keep my sanity, I had to give back the same way I lost.

KELLON

"Killa C," I yelled as I entered my Fathers chapel.

He turned around and glared at me. "I'll be happy when God strikes you down. What you want, boy?" Waving me off, he turned back towards the podium and grabbed his iPad.

"Just coming by to see if the old G wanted to go to lunch." I jumped out the way as he tried to punch me. "Mhm, that old age finally catching up to you." I teased but shut up once he gave that stern glare.

No matter how many years it has been, it still amazed me that Killa C, my Father, the once feared man in the streets, was now known as Bishop Cambridge of Evergreen Baptist Church. One of the largest congregations in South Florida that had more than five thousand consecutive members. After being hit with over ten bullets in a drive-by shooting and lived to tell it, he finally got the message God was sending him and changed his life.

"Nah, I ain't going to lunch with you. Now what you want?" I followed behind him as he locked up the church and sat down on a nearby bench near the parking lot.

Running a hand over my head, I prepared to tell my Father the same speech I was going to tell Orian, the head of Gump Records. "I'm not resigning with Gump. I decided to go independent and do my own thing."

"Does this have anything to do with that track you did with Drew Jones?" After Drew and I recorded the track two months ago, I sent it over to my pops for him to hear. He called me immediately and told me he loved it.

"Yeah. I'm not saying that's the lane I'll only be in, but that's what most of what my album would sound like." Drew Jones was what people considered a Christian rap artist. He rapped about God in all his lyrics but also mixed it with real life. He was taking over the charts with his music, and I knew the track he and I recorded would be a hit, or at least I hoped.

"I told you that I support whatever decision you made. What you need to ask yourself is if you are prepared to lose some fans. Lose money. I raised you to be smart with your money, so I know you're straight for life, but again, are you ready to lose your fame?" He stared me in my eyes searching for doubt or uncertainty.

He didn't find any because there wasn't any there. I was more than confident that I was going to be cool whether I sold out Madison Square Gardens or performed for a crowd of fifty.

"I'm prepared for it all. I meet with Orian in a few days. Then I also have the final meeting about the clothing line dropping in a month. Whether I never sell another album, I'm still making moves." I ran a hand over my head as I thought of Delilah and making sure that I would always be able to provide for her. I knew how to handle my finances. If I never made another album or stopped performing my pockets would be the same. Delilah was set for life.

He squeezed my shoulder and told me he was proud of me. "You have my support. I'm always going to support you especially with you out these streets." I nodded my head in agreeance. "How's my baby girl doing? She holding up okay?"

A gloomy cloud formed over my head. It was no secret to our close family and friends that we just had our third miscarriage. Hell, I for sure thought we were going to make a home run. However, unlike the two times before, this time was more painful. They actually had to do surgery and give her medication to cause her body to go into labor to deliver the baby.

"She's okay. We don't talk much about it. When we do, she shuts down and cries for hours. I know she fears that I'm going to leave her because she can't give me a baby, but I would never do that. Never even crossed my mind." I overheard her on the phone with Woody and the pain I felt from hearing her confession had me heated. I took each word of my vows seriously. In sickness and in health we were going to make it.

"Ever thought of adoption?"

"Funny you asked. I was reading about surrogates. Her eggs are fine, and my soldiers are marching. It's just finding the right person to carry the baby for us. She may not even go for it." The ache I felt realizing that I would never see my wife big and barefoot pregnant or watching her birth our children struck me. I told myself that I was okay, but was I really?

"What do you want? You have a say in the matter just as she does."

I opened my mouth to respond, but the black tinted out truck that crept into the parking lot grabbed my attention. At the same time, my Pops and I removed the heavy steel from our waist and propped it on our laps.

One thing I give my Pops, he never became naïve after becoming a man of the clergy. He stayed strapped in and out of the pulpit, and he dared any of his members to argue with him about it. Not to mention, he may not have been running the streets as he used to, but he was still involved with a lot of the lieutenants that ran his old stomping grounds.

The truck stopped a few feet from where he and I were parked. The passenger side door opened, and we clocked our guns. Seeing the pair of heels touch the pavement caused me to relax but then become angry.

I stretched out my legs and stared at Bianca as she made her way over to us. "As I was saying, Pops, to be honest with you, and I know it may sound selfish and crazy, but the kid thing has never been a top priority on my list. Yes, I want kids with my wife but at the same time if we don't ever have them, then I'm okay with that. It's only been hard to deal with because we created life and then boom, it was gone. So yeah, I hurt knowing that it may never be a possibility, but deep down I'm also okay with the latter. I'm too needy and stingy to share my wife with a dirty diaper baby anyway." He and I laughed.

"Hey, Bishop. What's up, KC?" Bianca batted her eyes and winked at me.

"What are you doing here, Bianca?" Pops cut straight to the chase.

Her eyes bounced between him and I before she smiled. "I came by to drop off the pamphlets for Sundays service." She handed him a thick folder. He took it from her not once breaking eye contact. When she finally realized what sat on both of our laps she gasped and stepped back.

"Thank you. Have a good day." He dismissed her, but she didn't move.

Bianca and I never had any dealings with each other. None. But that never stopped her from flirting with me every chance she got. If you weren't in relation to me, worked for me, or my wife, I paid you no mind. She worked for my Father, not me.

"How long are you in town for, KC? My girls and I went to your concert. I swear I almost melted when you performed 'You're Just My Type.' Had me thinking it was meant for me when you pointed out in the crowd." She bit her lip and twirled a strand of hair around her finger.

"Nah, that song is about and for *my* wife," I smirked when her eyes turned into slits.

Giggling nervously, she nodded. "Delilah was there too huh? That's cool. I guess I had a better advantage considering I *heard* the lyrics and she had to stand there and watch the rest of us hear that sexy voice of yours."

"Go about your business, Bianca." Pops gritted.

Shooting up to my full height, my piece of steel at my side causing her to back up. "What you say?"

Her eyes nervously watched my hand. "I-I...I"

"What you stuttering for? You had a mouth full to say a second ago." Taking a step closer, I watched her tremble. "Yo, I don't know what you thought, but you don't know me like that because if you did, then you would know that if there is anybody I don't play about it's my wife. You feel like you got leverage over her because you *heard* me rap at a concert? Understand something, Delilah is well acquainted with my voice. She hears it every time *I* dig deep into them guts."

Watching her mouth open to a full "O" made me smirk. Pops chuckled shaking his head. "I may not put my hands-on women, but I got a slew of cousins that will knock some sense in your ass. Around here opening your mouth to disrespect my wife like that. Matter of fact get to stepping." I waved her off and sat down. "I swear you broads ain't got no home training. What kind of people you got working in your church? She knows damn well I'm married but sashaying her ass in my face." I shook my head and watched the truck back out of the parking lot.

Pops sat laughing like what happened was funny. I didn't tolerate disrespect from anybody. My hands were itching to call one of my little cousins and have them tag team Bianca for a couple of bucks.

"Man, forget all that. Back to our conversation before your employee rudely interrupted." I removed the rolled blunt from behind my ear and sparked. Silently I asked God not to strike me for smoking on holy ground. I needed something to calm my nerves.

He held his hand out for me to pass it to him. "I was responding to you being spoiled. You've always been a special child that required more attention than most and Delilah made it worse by spoiling you."

"Hey," I shrugged my shoulders inhaling the smoke deep into my lungs. "I love my wife. I don't mind admitting that I'm clingy as hell when it comes to her." Anyone who knew me knew that I made no apologies when it came to Delilah. The only person I compromised with for her time was God, that's it.

My phone vibrated with a message from my lawyer telling me to check my email.

"How's that other situation coming along?" He was looking in the other direction, so I knew he didn't see my phone.

"I just got the email. I'm not ready for this." I groaned and held my head in my hands.

"All I know is, you better handle it like you got some sense. You know I don't play about my baby girl. You hurt baby; I'll hurt you." He didn't have to look me in the eyes for me to know that he was serious.

My Father played no games when it came to the women in his life. You could play with him all day, but not my Mother or Delilah.

"Pops, I'll holla at you later. I gotta go handle this." We hugged, and he threatened me to have Delilah at his house on Sunday for dinner. After promising that I would, I headed to my truck.

My hands trembled as I held my phone. With shaky fingers, I entered my passcode and went to my emails. The email from LabCorp was the first thing I saw. Clicking it open, I scanned the document until I read the results.

"Shit!" I threw my phone at the dashboard. Seeing the results awakened fear into my heart.

Delilah.

My eyes watered as I thought of what my life would be like without her in it. I already knew I was going to break her heart. With everything that we just went through this was the last thing I wanted to bring into our marriage, but I knew I had to tell her. I just prayed that she didn't leave me for it.

DELILAH

I stared at the face of Dr. Evelyn and reflected over the last twenty-eight years of my life. Was I a saint? Nope, not by far. Maybe that's why God was punishing me so because I made no attempts to live as the proverbs thirty-one woman. I mean, who did?

Not once have I stepped outside of my marriage, and my crazy infatuation with Morris Chestnut didn't count. He was the only man besides my husband that I ever had the droopy lustful eyes for. I mean come on. God knew exactly what he was doing when he created that beautiful chocolate bar of a man.

When we weren't on the road, I cooked, cleaned, did the laundry, and even went so far as to place my career of becoming a neonatal nurse on the back burner after we graduated college so that I could travel with him.

I was submissive in and out of the bedroom.

Per all eight acclaimed fertility specialists, my cervix was perfect. Eggs healthy. Kellon had a healthy and strong sperm count, but still, I was unable to carry to full term.

"Do you think it has anything to do with the car accident?" I asked as I shifted on the examination table.

Dr. Evelyn gave me a small smile. "No Delilah. You were twelve years old when that happened, and I've been your doctor since. No trauma to your reproductive system."

When I was twelve years old, I was in a car accident that killed my parents instantly. A drunk driver going the opposite direction veered off into our lane and hit us head-on. I suffered broken bones and lost seventy-five percent of my hearing in both of my ears from the impact.

After I was released from the hospital, I lived with my Grandmother Valerie until she passed when I was a freshman in college. My parents and grandmother were the only living family I had. Besides Woody, I had no family until I met Kellon and then his family welcomed me in as their own.

"So, what can I do? We've spent so much money and yet the results are all the same." I needed answers. Different answers other than the ones I've been given for the last five years.

"Have you ever thought about adoption or a surrogate?" She handed me a few pamphlets.

Shaking my head, I tried to control my emotions. Having another woman other than myself carry my husband's baby didn't sit well with me. In fact, it made my stomach queasy.

"No. Won't hurt to look these over I suppose." I placed them in my purse and stood. "Thank you for everything, Dr. Evelyn."

"It will get better, Delilah." She hugged me before escorting me out.

After a while, hearing that it would get better and other words of sentiment became static noise.

I wanted the better to happen now. I wanted to give my husband a child *now*. I wanted to walk around pregnant and have my sleep interrupted at three in the morning because my baby decided to use my womb as its personal playground.

The drive home was long. I took the long way to give me time to sit in my thoughts and prepare myself for the conversation Kellon and I needed to have. He could front and act like us not having kids didn't bother him, but I knew it did.

Today I received terrible news from both of my doctors. We weren't pregnant, and my last hearing test showed that I was losing complete hearing in my left ear. No one had explanations to any of my problems. None.

We paid a lot of money to be told 'I'm sorry, but we are unsure.'

When I pulled up in the driveway, the number of cars surprised me. It wasn't a surprise to see Khiver's car but seeing his lawyer and accountant's car surprised me.

I barely turned my key in the lock when the door opened. "Hey, sis." Khiver kissed my cheek.

Gathering my footing, I looked around. "Hey, Khi, what's with all the cars?"

Before he could answer, his brother called my name from down the hall. "Delilah." The bass of Kellon's voice caused my face to heat and cheeks to turn red. My lady parts had been silent all day. Hearing his voice woke her up and sent her into a frenzy.

I looked over Khiver's shoulder and met the intense gaze of Kellon. Looking into his eyes was like seeing him for the first time. I'll never forget how I felt when we first met. Our souls were talking. We were not involved in the manner. It felt like we were intruders invading a very intimate moment.

Standing tall with his legs gapped open, I admired the beautifully sculpted masterpiece. His chiseled features enhanced his dark milk chocolate skin. And those coal eyes had the power to increase my libido just by a sudden glare. A subtle, but intense glare that made my knees weak.

His healthy eating habits and dedicated workout regimen gave him a body that on most mornings he had to pry my limbs from around. Every ounce of Kellon was succulent.

With his index finger, he motioned for me to come to him. I tucked my lips in my mouth to stifle my purr. It had happened on a regular. My body purred for him at any given moment. From the smirk on his face, I failed at hiding it.

My steps faltered as my heart tumbled into the pit of my stomach. "Hi, babe."

With our height difference, whenever I kissed him, I shamelessly climbed him until I got in the position that I liked…deep in the crevice of his arms.

Staring at me with those intriguing eyes, he demanded me, "Kiss me." One hand wrapped firmly around my waist, holding me in place, and the other held my neck firm. "Stop playing," He smacked my booty. "You know what I want." I opened my mouth and stuck my tongue out. The minute his tongue touched mine I whimpered and melted into his chest.

When he first kissed me this way many moons ago, I thought he was into those kinky fetishes. Kellon liked to see his saliva run from his tongue onto mine and then he would suck my tongue until I creamed.

Weird, but I loved our weirdness.

The good prude girl I was before him had long ago vanished. I was ruined. He ruined me. He helplessly ruined me. Hopelessly was I devoted to him just as he was devoted to me. Irrevocably I was his as he was mine.

My lips pouted when he separated from me. His heavy chuckle caused my chest to vibrate. Kissing my nose, he promised me a happy ending. "I'll handle you later. Come on." He released my body and grabbed my hand.

As he walked towards the living room area, he turned and gave me a somber look. Something felt off. A voice in my head kept telling me to stop and go back outside. The closer we got, the faster my heart pounded.

I glanced down at his trembling hand that had become clammy. What was going on?

We turned the corner, and I gasped. It felt like I was hit in the chest by a large eighteen-wheeler with spiked wheels. My hand separated from Kellon's as I took in the woman sitting comfortably on my couch.

My head snapped up towards Kellon. "Why is she here?" My voice dripped with so much venom that I frightened myself.

No one said a word. Kellon seemed to forget how to speak. They all seemed to forget their words.

Taking a step further into the sitting area, I asked the million-dollar question. "Why are you here, Sasha?" I needed to know why the woman my husband cheated with was in my house.

KELLON

M y Father raised his sons to fear no man but God. All my life I
have never been frightened or scared of anything or anyone.
When I asked for Delilah's hand in marriage, I was nervous but not
scared. Even with my Father, I held a little fear, but it was a fear of
respect because of the position he played in my life. But this, watching
the anger boil in my wife's eyes had me scared shitless. My heart
pounded so hard that I felt the bruises forming on my chest cavity.

She hadn't said anything after she questioned why Sasha was in our
home. No one answered. It wasn't their responsibility to answer the
brandy eyed beauty. The burden was my own, and yet, I couldn't find the
strength to open my mouth and tell the truth.

Confess that my past transgression had finally caught up to me.

From the rapid blinking and the twist of her mouth, I knew Delilah
was overthinking. Thinking too hard about a situation that happened
before our vows.

"What's going on, Kellon?" Even though she spoke in a soft tone, I
knew better than to think she was calm.

"Hey, Delilah." I flinched at the greeting Sasha gave.

Out of the corner of my eye, I watched Khiver take small steps into
the sitting room. He and I both knew what transpired the last time these

two women were in the same vicinity of one another. Though Sasha's wave and greeting were innocent, Lilah didn't see it like that. Who would when the last time she saw her fists were flying and charges were pressed.

"How are you doing, Mrs. Cambridge?" My lawyer Chase stood.

It seemed the others in the room picked up on the shift of energy in the room. So much anger and animosity floated around making it stuffy and hard to breathe.

Seated amongst us in the room were my lawyer Chase, my accountant Jean, and my publicist Paige. My team that stayed ready and prepared to extinguish any fires I unintentionally caused.

"Seems I'm tardy for the party. It would be nice for someone to explain what is going on instead of greeting me like I haven't asked the same question twice." Delilah crossed her arms across her chest and began tapping her foot.

Before this got out of hand, I needed to calm my little lion. "Lilah, walk with me." Her head snapped towards me causing her hair to whip across her face. Her menacing glare chilled me, but I stayed firm in my glare. She tried to speak, but I gave her a look that made her mouth close. "Walk with me, Delilah," I spoke firmly. Holding out my hand, I waited for her.

She took one last look at the folks in our home and then placed her small hand on my large palm. With all the drama that was about to unfold, feeling her touch calmed me, unrattled my nerves, and gave me the confidence to hope that this would go smoother than I projected.

Instead of taking her to my office down the hall I opted for our bedroom. Our oasis. Our haven of peace. Our place of comfort and tranquility. The place we spent hours on our knees in prayer fighting. Not just for one another and our marriage, but for our family, friends, my career. All of the above.

The place that she unselfishly submitted to me and let me drive her to realms of ecstasy that it took days for us to come down from our love-making high.

To others, I may seem coldhearted, but to my wife, she never experienced anything but respect, and I wasn't about to change that by blindsiding her with my bad news in front of others. Bad enough she had to see Sasha before I could tell her the truth.

With watchful eyes, I watched with desire as she removed her blazer and then her pumps. As each article of clothing fell from her body, the purpose of me bringing her up here got pushed back into my head and thoughts of making love to my wife raced to the front.

Thinking of making love to Delilah gave me the idea that I could tell her of my errored ways while I was deep in her cave of warmth. She'd forgive me. She'd still love me. She wouldn't leave. I'd make sure of it. I'd make sure that each stroke removed any hurt and pain I caused. I'd replace the hurt with love, but I couldn't do that. After the sex high wore off, she'd be even more upset that I used sex to hurdle her emotions.

Taking a seat next to her on our bed, I grabbed her hand and ran my fingers over her ring. "Sasha is here because there was a paternity test done on her eight-year-old son Kiser." Taking a deep breath, I revealed the truth. "He's mine, Lilah."

I got into my first fist fight at the age of eight. I went knuckle to knuckle with dudes that were twice my size. No man placed fear in my heart, but the silence of this woman sitting next to did.

The silence around us strangled me. Prying my eyes from our joined hands, I took the last bit of courage I had and looked into her eyes. What I saw caused my heart to sink.

Emptiness.

There was nothing in her eyes as she stared straight ahead. She looked soulless. Her body didn't stiffen. None of the emotions I prepared myself to receive from her were given.

Pure agonizing silence.

"Sa-Sasha reached out to me a month ago. She's not here for money. After all these years she thought Kiser was her husbands' child. It wasn't until he became severely sick from Lupus that they found out. She had all her children tested for the gene. He doesn't have it, but her other two sons do. The question of why Kiser didn't have it and the other kids did led to a DNA test." My heart pounded faster and harder as the seconds ticked by.

Delilah said nothing. No tears. Just a blank expression.

Finally, she turned towards me. Even though her eyes were on me, she wasn't there. "What's the plan?" She asked lowly.

I ran a hand over my head as I exhaled. "We had a DNA test done a week ago." The long breath she released caught me off guard. We never had secrets. I communicated everything. I knew she felt like I betrayed her by keeping this from her for so long.

"I-I...we agreed on joint custody. As I said, she doesn't want a ridiculous amount of child support. We both want me to get to know him and move forward." I rubbed a hand over my chest. The thought of Lilah not accepting Kiser escalated my anxiety. I prayed she didn't place me in a situation to choose between her and my son.

My hand dropped from her lap as she stood. "I guess we should go back downstairs and get the ball rolling." I reached my hand out to stop her but dropped it when she shot me a glare.

With each step that I took down the stairs, I cursed myself for my stupidity. I never cheated during our marriage. Not once have I had thoughts of giving another woman what was only for my wife. But I did, however, cheat at the beginning of our relationship when we started dating.

Eyes watched intently as Delilah sat opposite of everyone at the dining table. I knew she was strong enough to handle anything, but I wanted a reaction.

Chase and Jean went over the joint custody agreement and the monthly child support. It seemed like everything happened in a blur. I half listened with most of my focus on Delilah. She said nothing. Never asked questions or gave her thoughts on the matter. When it was revealed that Kiser was coming here for the summer next week I searched her face for a reaction.

Again, I got nothing.

The more Chase spoke, the more I felt like a complete asshole for not only blindsiding her with the news but not talking with her alone about the situation before everything was pretty much set in stone. I'll admit, I thought taking care of everything before getting Delilah involved would soften the blow. She would have to go along with everything because it had been handled.

After the paperwork was signed, that eerie silence encompassed everyone. Sasha was looking at Lilah who was staring at the DNA test laying in the middle of the table.

Khiver must have read my thoughts. He escorted himself and everyone out of our home. I went to lock up the house and came back to an empty table. I followed her scent up the stairs and into our bedroom. Following the trail of clothes, I went into our bathroom and watched her from behind the foggy glass.

I had to do something. Our connection was breaking, and I needed to bring her back in. Stripping out my clothes, I swallowed my pride and opened the glass shower door. Before I could place a foot inside, she said one word that caused my heart to drop. Looking me dead in the eye she said, "Grace."

In the seven years that we have been married that word has only been used twice.

When we first got married, we both agreed that we needed a safe word that would represent when we needed to table a discussion before words were spoken that neither of us meant. Our tempers mixed didn't benefit anyone. Both of our mouths were lethal when pushed to a certain point. The situations became dark and ugly.

Before an argument could escalate, the safe word was said, and then we would table it and come back once we got ahold of our emotions and could speak respectfully with understanding.

The first time the word was used was by her. It happened right after our first miscarriage. I wanted to talk about it. Get inside her head. See what she was feeling. Instead, she used the safe word and shut me out.

Now, here we were years later, and she did the same thing. But this time I couldn't blame her. She knew how much I loved communicating and talking things through. When she and I were at odds, it changed my entire mood. If it was anyone else I couldn't care less, but this was my wife. The love of my life. The woman I loved more than anything and she safe worded me.

Picking up my clothes, I showered in the bathroom across the hall. We could shower separate, but we weren't going to sleep separate, and I hope she knew that.

When I walked back into the bedroom, she was laying on her side of the bed facing the window. It's hard to explain the relief of seeing her laying in our bed. We could fight all day, but our bed, her in my arms, mad or not, she was going to lay with me.

I felt my spirit brighten just a tad as I pulled her into my chest. I squeezed her tight and wrapped her deep in the crevice of my arms just the way she liked. It didn't take long before the first body wave of shuttering happened followed by a mountain of tears. I did the only thing I could do. I held her tight and promised that I'd fix my mess.

DELILAH

Growing up as a teenager not being able to hear without the help of my hearing aid, I became grateful for the silence I could provide myself when the voices around me seemed too loud. I never used my disability as a means to seek attention or have a pity party. In fact, I saw the beauty in it. Some people were born deaf and would never hear the voices of their loved ones. I, on the other hand, experienced years of hearing voices and sounds.

Though I had a small percentage of hearing left, it equaled to low whispers. People still had to yell for me to understand what they were saying clearly. Being able to sit in my thoughts became a favorite of mine. Kellon hated when I went without my hearing aid or turned it off purposely. No matter how many times I told him I enjoyed reading his lips, he still preferred that I heard his voice. Like now.

I watched with annoyance as he eyed my hearing aid laying on the dresser. He had to be out of his mind if he thought I would put it in to hear him apologize over and over again. Not a chance. I wasn't going to budge one bit.

My eyes drifted down to the black socks on his feet. Up to his toned calves and muscled legs. My bottom lip disappeared between my teeth as I marveled over his black briefs that enhanced my favorite lover below. I continued my inspection up his sculpted abs, to his two protruding pecs. My self-will was fighting to hold on as I eyed the Arabic script across his left pec that translated to my name.

Moving up his thick neck to his lips, I couldn't help but snicker at the snarl he gave me. His hands raised and his fingers began moving. Unlike my grandmother, God rest her soul, he had perfected the craft of sign language.

I remember it like it was yesterday. While I was waiting for him to break up with me because of my disability, he was going to sign language classes on the low. The first full sentence he signed to me was I love you. I knew right then that I never wanted to be without this man. The intimacy we shared by not speaking but through signed words was an experience I cherished over sending flirty texts throughout the day.

My brow arched as he fussed at me through his sign language. Oh, he was big mad.

To be honest, I don't know how I felt about the news Kellon dropped on me about having a child with my nemesis Sasha. All night, Kellon consoled me as I cried well into the wee hours of the morning. With the vibrations coming from his chest as he held me I knew he was apologizing.

None of that mattered. He could save the apologies.

"I'm not putting it back in." I finally spoke. Turning towards the large bay window overlooking Florida's intercoastal I gathered my thoughts. "I don't want to hear you explain something that I have been trying to tell you for years."

I chuckled in disbelief. Out of all the women in the world he had to make a baby with it had to be Sasha. I knew about the cheating. He confessed right after he did it. He promised never to do it again, and to my knowledge that was the last time. Or was it?

How could he expect me to trust me when he waited a whole month and DNA test later to tell me he fathered a child with the bride of Chucky?

"Kellon, you are…you are sooo naïve. I want to say you are stupid or ignorant, but I have too much respect for you to say those words, so I'm going to use naïve." Closing my eyes, I pinched the bridge of my nose.

"That woman has been a thorn in my ass for the last eight years. She's haunted my dreams and always had this unspoken clout in our marriage. In my relationship with you."

My anger was getting the best of me as I turned around and pointed a finger in his face. "When she popped up pregnant years ago I told you to have a DNA test done. But no," I tossed my hands in the air. "You swore up and down that it wasn't yours. Said there was no way in hell that her baby was yours. You were so worried that you were going to lose me that you became blind and ignorant to the fact that all it takes is one time to father a child.

Sasha knows damn well what she was doing, and you'll be a bigger fool to believe that the innocent woman sitting on my couch yesterday has changed from the psycho possessed chic she was years ago." I moved closer to him until our chests touched.

I knew he was furious. I read the words from his lips. He didn't like people in his personal space but so what.

"She sent me emails with sonograms and notes from the doctor every chance she got. Pushed it in my face daily." Mustering up some strength, I pushed him. "I came to you time and time again about it. You ignore me. Now, look where that got us, your whore in my house drinking my juice telling us when we can and can't see your *son*."

I waited for my body to calm down slowly. "My heart and feelings are numb right now, Kellon, so excuse me for not showing the emotions you want. I cried last night because I'm tired, Kellon. So tired. I've placed my career on hold for you because you wanted me to travel with you. I settled to be a baby rocker."

My legs became wobbly as I stepped back from him. His scent was suffocating. "Seeing her yesterday broke something in me. What, I don't know. But it broke, and I know this because I began to form a hatred towards you for allowing this to happen."

Dropping down onto the bed, I buried my head in my hands. Our safe word was on the tip of my tongue, but I knew I couldn't run from our problems forever.

Looking up into his eyes the dam that had been locked away had a crack in it. My eyes watered as I watched the rim of his eyes flood with tears. My strong protector was breaking right along with me.

"You are my husband. My provider. The man who is supposed to keep me safe and protect me. Yesterday, a month ago, eight years ago, you didn't do that. Your actions of selfishness didn't protect me. Protect my," I covered my mouth as my voice cracked with heavy emotion. "Protect my heart from the pain I feel.

You've been living carefree for years while I knew deep down that there was a strong possibility that Sasha's child could be yours. You took her getting married as a sign that it wasn't yours." My body shook with anger as I chuckled at his stupidity.

"Bump that; you are stupid for thinking just because she married someone else that the child's DNA would miraculously change. As a man, wouldn't you want to know if another man was raising your son? What about their beliefs? They probably got the poor boy around here thinking Kanye West is Jesus." I rolled my eyes and wiped my face.

"None of that ran through your head? Damn, you are so selfish. Now I must find it in my heart to love an innocent child. A child that didn't come from my womb but the womb of the woman you cheated on me with!" Even though I couldn't hear myself speak loud enough, I knew my yelling surprised him. "I have to decide if I'm ready to accept the fact that Kiser may be the only child because we both know I can't carry any."

Out the corner of my eye, I watched his mouth move. I heard his voice that came through as mumbled whispers. I didn't want to know what he had to say. I got everything off my chest, and the only thing I wanted to do was sleep this headache away. Scooting back, I settled on my side and turned away from him. My eyes had barely closed before I felt the bed dip and a heavy weight on top of me.

Kellon gathered my hands above my head and held them firm with one hand. With the other, he turned my head and placed my hearing aid in. Seeing the sadness in those coal eyes dug the sting in my chest deeper. I almost felt bad for him.

"Delilah, baby, please forgive me. I'm sorry for hurting you, but you can't shut me out. We are in this together. You and I." I squeezed my eyes shut to block my tears from betraying me. "Lilah, I can fix this. Please forgive me. I'm sorry, baby." With each apology, his grip loosened until I was free.

He didn't move from on top of me. He continued to apologize while I lay immobile wishing I'd wake up from this nightmare.

KELLON

My brother Khiver and I were only two years apart. He's been my manager since I started rapping. There were no questions asked if I wanted him to manage me or not. It was either him or my Father. Growing up, he had dreams of working in the music industry. I gave him the key to walk into his goals by using my gift to open doors that neither of us imagined would open. Not only was he managing me, but also a few other big-time artists. Khiver was living his dream to the fullest.

Since I was a young boy, I witnessed love in its most accurate humanly form. It began with my grandparents and then my parents. Seeing passion so raw, uncut, authentic, and real, I knew what I wanted to be, and that was a good man for the right woman. Never had an interest of becoming a doctor, lawyer, or athlete. I wanted to be the best husband I could be.

Rapping was my calling. My purpose. I touched people with my words. Planted the seeds and God watered them. I was doing what I was created to do. Touch people with my rhymes. My passion was to be a devoted husband to my wife.

Watching the rise and fall of her chest, I couldn't help but feel like I failed at that one job.

Like any morning, I started my day out by standing by the large bay window near our bed watching Delilah sleep. I wasn't on no creep shit. It had become a habit since the first time she laid in my arms. I rose early just for this moment. Watching her sleep and talking to God was my dose of morning coffee.

Even when I was on the road, it was the same thing. If we were apart, which wasn't often, I stared at the hundreds of pictures I had of her in my phone.

Last night I felt defeated. I battled with being angry at Delilah and myself. She never spoke with so much malice or said things she didn't mean, so I knew that was precisely how she truly felt.

Standing, I walked over to her side of the bed and watched her carefully. I missed Delilah. Missed her a lot.

How could I miss someone who laid inches from me? Who shared the same bed? Who lived under the same roof?

Easy.

A week and a half had passed since I last touched my wife. I tried to. Lord knows I have, but she moves out of my grasp. I missed her touch. Missed the feel of her lips. Missed hearing her laugh. Missed her river of love drowning around me. Besides her allowing me to hold her at night, that was all she allowed me to do.

Leaning down, I pushed a curl back and ran the back of my hand over her cheek. The moan that escaped her lips had me ready to toss the covers off her body and remind her of what we shared. Get us back to where we were before our world got turned upside down.

"I'll be back," I whispered against her lips.

I started to move back but was stopped by her arm circling my neck. She pulled me back down and pecked my lips until it was I who moaned. "I love you," She spoke softly. Without opening her eyes, she kissed me one last time and turned over.

Walking out to my truck, I couldn't help but smile like I won the lottery. Delilah wasn't one who held grudges or held onto negative feelings. Once she said her peace, that was it. She moved on. After the death of her parents, she learned how short life was. She had a thing for making sure that regardless of how she felt, she would tell you she loved you. She wanted the last words exchanged to be words of endearment.

So yeah, I may have been smiling prematurely cause she and I still had a lot of work to do, but it was a start.

"**Y**ou want me to cave your chest in now or after I call my baby girl?" Khiver and I both stepped back from my Father. "Nah, step back up here." The deep bass of his voice echoed through the church.

"Pops, come on man," I groaned and took another step back when he moved closer.

"Did I raise you to not handle your responsibilities as a man? Uh, did I not?" His eyes widened with each word he yelled. This wasn't Bishop Cambridge. This was Killa C from Driftwood.

"I-I didn't..."

"Where is my baby girl? I hope she left you for being so damn stupid." He sucked his teeth and pulled out his phone. "Baby girl, call me when you get this message." He hung up the phone and pointed at me. "You better be glad it went to voicemail." It was no secret that Delilah held a special place in my Father's heart. She was the daughter that my parents never had. They spoiled her rotten.

Khiver stood behind me snickering. "Aye, don't shoot me. I ain't the one in trouble." I waved him off and sat on the front pew.

"What am I supposed to do? Delilah flipped on me last week. I ain't never seen my baby like that." I rubbed the burning spot on my chest trying to take the ache away.

"Uh, well actually, you have. It was the night she and Sasha got into that big fight after your concert in New York. How could you forget? That was the night she caught you with Sasha, and apparently the night my nephew was conceived." Khiver thought my personal problems were funny.

"I thought you had a meeting with Orian?" Pops asked.

Meeting with Orian was the least of my worries now. "I rescheduled it. This is more important."

"Son, I won't sit here and say that I'm not disappointed in you because I am. I'm disappointed in you for pushing the fact that that boy may be yours under the rug like he was going to disappear. You were having sex with that girl, so you knew it could've been yours. I'm upset because you let another man raise your child because you didn't want to be a responsible adult. Your lack of responsibility hurt more than that child. It hurt your wife." He paced back and forth shaking his head and pulling on his beard.

"I feel bad for Delilah the most," Khiver said. "Can you imagine what is going through her head right now? She lost another baby a month ago, and now she finds out the chick you used to creep with had your son. You know how women feel about giving their man their first son." He looked at me and then shook his head.

"Why you wait until Sasha was at your house to tell her about the paternity test anyway? That was fucked up." Khiver glared at me.

I opened my mouth to speak, but the force of my Fathers' fist to my chest knocked the wind out of me. "Got me acting a fool in the Lord's house. You really were on some disrespectful bullshit, huh? Around here cussing like I'm out in the streets. I can't believe you, Kellon!" He barked with spit flying from his mouth.

Heck, I can't believe he just punched me in my chest.

I flinched when he marched and stood in my face. "Listen to me good. Never let your wife be the last to know anything. Anything, Kellon. You knew about this boy for over a month. I knew. Your brother knew. Delilah should've known as soon as Sasha called. Stop trying to hide things from her thinking you're keeping her from leaving you because all you're going to do is put yourself in a position to being alone from all your lies. You can't make her stay, son. Hiding the truth won't keep her. It will only push her away."

Everything he said was the truth. I ignored or pretended that Sasha's baby wasn't mine because I didn't want to lose Delilah. I hid everything that has happened over the last month because I didn't want her to think she could divorce me.

"Now stand up." Pops stood up in front of me with his arms open. I gave him the side eye and waved him off. "Boy, if you don't hug your old man." Mumbling under my breath, I stood and hugged him. "I love you, Kellon. Always will. But you hurt my baby girl, so I had to hurt you. Fix this."

"Awe, this is such a kodak moment." Khiver took out his phone and started taking pictures.

"Oh, don't think I ain't coming for you, Casanova. Wanna tell me why out of all the single women in my congregation you had to mess with Deacon White's daughter?" When Khiver's jaw dropped, I knew that was my cue to exit.

"I'm gone. Take it easy on him, Pops."

I had to come up with a way to fix the damage I caused. Divorce wasn't an option. Delilah wasn't leaving me, and she knew that. A blind man would know that. This was forever.

DELILAH

I should've been surprised to receive a call from Sasha but I wasn't. I should've been surprised when she asked if she and I could sit down and talk. When I prayed for God to direct me with this situation I knew I would have to come face to face with her. The thirty-minute pep talk I gave myself on the drive here helped calm my nerves. I was open-minded. Technically I had no choice but to be open-minded.

"Delilah, I first want to apologize about everything. I was childish back then. Please forgive me for all the heartache I caused." Her apology didn't move me. It ticked me off more.

"You mean for the heartache that you are still causing?" I titled my head and squinted my eyes. Yeah, I know I prayed for my attitude to be checked at the door, but I couldn't stand the ground that Sasha walked on.

Her head dropped. When she lifted her head up, she had the nerve to have tears building up in her eyes. "I'm sorry. Back then I was a stupid girl chasing a check and a man that didn't want me."

"But you still chasing the check, Sasha. Did you and Kellon just not agree on an amount for child support? Did his lawyer not retract it back to the day Kiser was born? You can save those tears for someone else who cares and doesn't know the real you." I motioned for the waiter to place my order.

If I was going to have to sit through this circus, I couldn't be sober.

"I-I met my husband a month after I found out I was pregnant. Kellon never once denied his love for you and that night at the hotel…I-I came up with a plan b and that was to convince my husband that the baby was his." She picked up a napkin and dabbed her eyes. My eyes were guaranteed to be stuck in my head by the time she finished her sob story.

"My secret lasted for years. It wasn't until Will took a turn for the worse with his Lupus. As a precaution we got all the boys tested. My twin sons have it but not Kiser. It was then that I revealed my big secret. To my surprise, Will knew all along. Not once has he ever treated Kiser any different." By now the faucet to her waterworks had turned on. I sat back, sipped my wine, and shook my head.

"Please forgive me for bringing drama into your marriage. I know we can never be friends," I snorted and giggled. Was this chick serious? "I hope we can be cordial for the sake of Kiser and Kellon."

Closing my eyes, I took several deep breathes to calm myself. She wanted to be cordial. Cordial. I wanted her out my life for good, but there was no way that could happen.

"Tell me about Kiser." I had to shift gears here. Her melodramatic performance was worse than nails scraping against a chalkboard.

Her eyes lit up as she started telling me about my step-son.

Wow.

Step-son.

I had a step-son

"He's such a smart kid. He really is. Before he knew about Kellon, he was already a fan of his music. All my boys are." She reached into her purse and retrieved her phone. "The older he gets, the more he looks like Kellon. Here, he looks more like Khiver."

It was on the tip of my tongue to ask if he was a possible candidate of being his father, but I remembered, Kellon had already been proven to be the father.

"Wow," I breathed out slowly. There was no denying Kiser. He was the spitting image of his father.

My hands shook as I tried to get ahold of my emotions. This was happening. This was really happening.

The more I tried to wrap my brain around the fact that Kellon had an outside child the harder my heart hardened. If I knew this was a possibility all along why was I crumbling? Was it because I acted just as foolish as Kellon? Hoping and praying that it never came true.

"Kiser has this infatuation with NASCAR's. He has a large collection of model cars around his room..." Sasha's bragging about her child caused my head to become cloudy.

I wasn't sure of what to do or what to think. My heart was bleeding and becoming hardened by the second. It's like the blood from my heart were my tears that mixed with Kellon's dirt of lies and formed a thick layer of brick.

"Excuse me," I darted from the table and rushed to the bathroom.

Closing the door and locking it, I slid down until I came to a squat. My chest heaved up and down as I started dry crying. My insides were crying. My heart cried. My eyes, however, were bare of moisture. My body shook as if I were.

What had I done so wrong in life for me to suffer like this? Was this the wages of my sins? Who did I piss off?

Nothing made sense.

All I ever want to do was fulfill my duty as a woman. I married the man of my dreams. I supported his career. I sexed him from the mountaintops. Yet the one thing that is expected of me, I can't do. How can I even consider myself useful when I can't reproduce?

I am a woman. We are baby making machines. So, why? Why did Sasha's womb open and produce a child for my husband but mine won't?

Standing, I walked over to the sink and splashed water on my face. I'm glad no tears did appear because the last thing I wanted to do was give Sasha an inclination that she affected me.

With my head held high, I walked out and sat back down. Her mouth picked up where it left off and began running like a motor. I caught bits and pieces of what she was saying but ignored most of it. Nothing grabbed my attention until she stepped over her boundaries.

"You never wanted children, Delilah?"

"Stay in your lane, Sasha. This ain't that type of party nor will it ever be." I motioned for the waitress and asked for my bill. "Listen, out of respect for my husband and his son I will be cordial, but other than that we do not need to communicate. I'm sure all communication regarding Kiser will be done between you and Kellon. With that being said, unlike how you acted years prior, respect my marriage and understand that Kellon is a married man now and his wife is batshit crazy. Enjoy the rest of your day."

As soon as my car door closed, I yelled out in anger and frustration. Beat up on my steering wheel until my knuckles hurt. Kicked until I stubbed my toe on the brake pedal. Not even that hurt enough to distract me from the pain in my heart.

KELLON

Staring at someone is often considered rude. Burning a whole into their face. Analyzing their features. Forming your own assumption about them just based off what your eyes told you. When I stared at Delilah, I lost myself. My thoughts became clear. Focused aligned with purpose. The gateways of those brandy eyes brought me back from giving up on many occasions.

We were at our friend's house enjoying a relaxing Saturday out on their back porch. Music played in the background. Smoke from the barbeque grill caused my stomach to stick to my back. Laughter and smiles were on everyone's faces, but not mine. Instead, I sat back on the lounge chair and stared at my forever obsession.

My Delilah.

"Delilah, you can move in. The bedroom next to the nursey is yours. Just say the word, and Orian will have your stuff moved in before the sun sets," Heather whined as she sat next to her husband. "This is the first time in days that he has sat quietly. Gosh, I need you to rub your baby magic on me."

Delilah giggled and cuddled baby Orian closer to her chest. "I wish I could, but I can't leave my big baby like that." She turned and winked at me. I dipped my head to hide my red cheeks.

"I know that grown man over there is not blushing?" Orian teased.

Heather playfully hit his arm. "Leave him alone, baby. They are the most adorable couple ever. Such relationship goals. Orian, you better make me smile like Delilah when we reach seven years. Y'alls love is so potent."

I studied Lilah's face as she glanced over at me. If only people knew what type of demons we were facing behind these smiles.

For the past hour, I've sat back and watched Delilah hold and comfort colicky Orian Jr. Heather called this morning in tears because she couldn't get him to stop crying. I loved seeing Lilah in action when it came to her nurturing babies, so I asked to tag along. In truth, it was my excuse to be near her.

Delilah knew how much I loved having attention. Her attention. She was depriving me of her attention, and I didn't like that. Our issues hadn't been squared away, but damn. How much longer was she going to keep her love from me?

"Can't believe you're leaving me after all these years. I saw it coming, though. I'm proud of you for stepping out on your own." When we arrived at their house, I pulled Orian to the side and told him that I wasn't going to resign with him. We shook hands, and he wished me the best. There was no bad blood between us. Never had been.

"He fell asleep. Repeat everything you saw me do, and he should be fine. If not, call me. Hmm, goddies baby is so precious." Delilah rubbed her nose against the baby's cheek and sniffed him.

"Wait, before you go, Orian and I want to talk to you both about something." Heather looked at Orian and smiled. He grabbed her hand and kissed her cheek.

Delilah turned to me with questionable eyes. I shrugged my shoulders because I had no clue what they wanted to talk to us about.

Heather sat up straight and smiled at Delilah. "Orian and I have been thinking and praying about how we are going to help a family in need this year. Usually, we pay a family's mortgage for a year, remodel houses, send a few kids to college, or whatever it is that God places on our hearts."

She reached over and placed her hand on Lilah's knee. "We would like to know if you would give us the honor of caring your baby for you?" Both of our mouths opened in surprise.

Delilah had been hardcore about her feelings the past few weeks so seeing her overcome with emotion shocked me. She sat with baby Orian in her arms as the tears poured down her face.

"I can't imagine the pain and trauma you've had to endure these last couple of years, Delilah. The baby would, of course, be you all's fertilized egg. The only thing we ask is that you make us Godparents. Orian Jr. is four months old. I spoke with my doctor about it, and she told me that I'm in perfect health to be a surrogate for you." Heather beamed with a bright smile.

Delilah sat in the same position with her mouth open. Speaking for the both of us I said the only thing I could say, "Thank you." For Heather to want to sacrifice her body for us meant a lot.

"Babe, I think you caused the poor woman to go into shock." Orian chuckled as he grabbed his son from Delilah's arms.

She hadn't moved. She sat there and cried silently. Seeing her overcome with emotion caused my own eyes to water. Babies, in general, had been a touchy subject. I questioned her motive for continuing to work at the hospital. Her reason was simple. It healed her.

"Think about it, okay, Delilah?" Heather pulled her into her arms. Lilah nodded and squeezed Heather tighter.

"Thank you. I appreciate everything." I shook hands with Orian.

"We're family. Just because you aren't signed under me anymore doesn't mean our brotherhood is over. You're my kid's godfather. We'll always help out in any way that we can." Orian said as he and Heather walked us to the door.

"Call me later, okay?" Heather pulled Delilah into another hug before she got in the car. Still overwhelmed, she gave a small smile and nodded her head.

"Have a good night." I waved as I backed out their driveway.

We sat in silence as I drove home. My hands kept flexing in a fist. I wanted to console Delilah. Wipe away her tears. Tell her that everything was going to be okay. Something prevented me from doing it, so I sat silent and listened to her sniffle.

All I wanted was for Lilah to talk to me. Besides that one day when she flipped and went off on me, she hadn't said much of anything. She didn't even tell me that she and Sasha had lunch. Sasha was the one who told me. I commended her for reaching out, but at the same time, I didn't. It's like she used her sympathy to poke the bear.

I placed my truck in park and watched as she got out and walked to the door. She didn't even wait for me. Closing my eyes, I gave myself time to relax and get my mind right. Two people with attitudes about two different issues weren't going to solve anything. The silent treatment had to stop.

Tonight.

The end of us not talking or me not being able to touch her ended now.

"Damn it, man." I groaned as my phone rung. I snatched it out my pocket and grinned. "What's up, little man?"

"Hey, Kellon, are you busy?" For an eight-year-old kid, Kiser had a lot of bass in his voice.

I glanced up at the empty staircase and shook my head. "Nah, I'm not busy. What's up?"

"I just wanted to check and see if you were still coming this weekend? Mom and I already packed my bags." The excitement in his voice brightened my mood.

A warm feeling settled in my chest as I thought of what our first reaction would be meeting each other face to face. "I'll be there Saturday morning. Are you excited? You aren't afraid of planes, are you?"

"Are you kidding? I love planes. Not as much as I love cars, but it's close." I laughed at his high level of energy. "I'm excited to spend my summer in Florida. Can't wait to go to the beach. Will Mrs. Delilah be spending time with us as well? I hope she likes me. Do you think she'll like me? I have a cool gift for her. Mom helped me pick it out."

I glanced up and eyed our closed bedroom door. "Yeah, Mrs. Delilah will be here. She's really nice. You'll love her."

"That's cool. Okay, well I have to go. Call me before you fly out. Talk to you later, Kellon."

"Later, Kiser." I hung up the phone and started my journey upstairs.

When I reached our bedroom, it was empty. I checked the bathroom, and it was also empty. The beat of my heart could be heard loud and clear through my ears.

Did she leave me?

I checked her reading room. Empty. Bathrooms empty. Kitchen empty. I was still standing by the front door while I was on the phone so how did she get past me?

Remembering that I had cameras all over the house, I went into my office and pulled up the security cameras. "Damn it, Lilah." I exhaled as I watched her stand in the middle of the floor in one of the spare bedrooms.

Taking the stairs two at a time, I opened the door slowly. Standing behind her, I took in the newly decorated room. Gone was the Egyptian baby theme and replaced with NASCAR's.

"Sasha said that he likes Nascars. Woody came over, and her design team redecorated the room yesterday." Her shoulders violently shook. "His favorite books, video games, and," The more she spoke, the harder she cried. "His favorite movies are all here. I hope he likes it."

I reached out and wrapped my arms around her just in time as her knees buckled. Slowly, our bodies dropped to the floor. Wrapping my arms and legs around her body, I held her tight as she cried. Her cries turned into pitiful wails. This cry wasn't just about her accepting Kiser or Sasha. This was the cry she had been holding in from all the pain and suffering we encountered over the years.

This cry held the pain of the first child we lost. The second. The third. It held the pain of her not pursuing her dreams of becoming a nurse. It contained the pain of my lies and deceit. This cry held the dirt as her soul cleansed itself.

"Lilah, I love you. I love you more than anything. We are stronger than our troubles. Together we can overcome anything. Together we can fight together. Baby, let me in. Let me in, Delilah. Your pain is my pain. Give me your burdens, Lilah. Give me your pain, and I promise tomorrow will be a brighter day. Let go and let me, Lilah. I love you so much. So much, Mama. You have no idea how much I love you."

DELILAH

I'm a fool.

    I'm crazy.

I've gone mad.

With the love I have in heart for Kellon 'KC' Cambridge, I'm afraid that I have gone mad.

I feel bamboozled. He tricked me. Kellon Cambridge played me, and I fell for it.

After the night that I cried a river in the middle of my step-sons room, I held Kellon to his word. He promised me a brighter tomorrow if I gave him my pain. That was three days ago, and this stupid smile plastered on my face had hardened and wouldn't go away.

His shirt was still draped over my body. His socks still clothed my feet. His boxers even warmed my booty.

He bamboozled me into giving up the draws. Well, he hadn't taken them yet, but I was two point three seconds away from begging him to have his way with me.

That made me giggle. The idea of me taking it. His nasty behind would love it.

"Keep staring at me like that, and you gon get what you looking for," he spoke without lifting his head from his book bag as he packed light for his turn around trip.

I sat in the middle of our bed in my feelings. He was leaving in a few hours to go to Dallas to get Kiser. Part of me wanted to tag along, but the other part of me, the petty part, said I needed to sit down and behave. Besides, this was Kellon's first time meeting his son. I was taking baby steps with my new approach to acceptance. Seeing my husband's reflection in childlike form wasn't something I could stomach at the moment. I still had another full day to get my mind right.

We hadn't been intimate in a while. An all-time new for us. It wasn't that I didn't desire his touch. It was the complete total opposite. My soul set ablaze on fire for him. I yearned for him more than I usually did. I ached for this man in sleep.

Maybe the increase in my desire came from the fight my soul and spirit were in. They knew the inner battle I was trying to pull by distancing myself from Kellon. It was a tug of war on my heart and I was losing. I wanted to stay in my pain and let it consume me, but my soul and spirit weren't having that. They were fighting against me and had entirely become #teamkellon.

I got so lost in my thoughts that I hadn't paid attention to when he moved in front of me. His presence suffocated me but in a good way. I liked not being able to breathe because he breathed for me.

Staring into his orbs, it didn't take long for me to get lost. His dark coal eyes were compelling, magnetic. I ignored the hitching of my breath and focused on the fact that it had been weeks since I felt the touch of my husband. I desired him. I needed him.

He studied me as I studied him. He knew what I was feeling. If he didn't, then my pheromones surly told him so. When his eyebrows raised, I knew I had confirmed his suspicion.

For a long moment, he gazed at me with such intensity that I moaned. There was an unspoken invitation in the simmering depths of his eyes.

"Come to me." His voice was calm, his gaze steady, but tone demanding.

I shook my head and scooted back further onto the bed. "N-Nope." Stand your ground, Delilah; I coached myself.

Listen, I never denied my husband my body. Never. It hurt me more than him to deny him, but I knew what was about to happen. My honeypot below twitched because she knew what he was capable of. Kellon Cambridge was a passionate lover. Selfish in the sense that my pleasure, me reaching peak after peak, was his undoing.

He cocked his head to the side and pinned me down with his chilling stare. "Why won't you come to me, Lilah?" His voice was so thick and husky. No man on this planet should have a voice that deep.

I pulled my legs up to my chest and nibbled on my bottom lip. Kellon walked over and turned off the lights. The only light illuminating the room came from the sun coming through the large bay window.

Back and forth he paced stripping off layer after layer. Damn, he didn't play fair.

"Kh-Khiver will be here soon." The tremble in my voice had nothing to do with fear or being afraid. It was from me not being able to control my hormones as this Adonis stood before me naked as the day he was born.

"Lilah, I want to feel you, baby. You don't want to feel me?" His eyes were on me. Eyes that watched me drool as I became hypnotized by the movement of his hand moving back and forth on my favorite lover. "Delilah, come to me." When he spoke again, his voice was tender, almost like a murmur but the demand was loud and clear.

"Why are you so demanding?" I teased. "And, no, I won't come to you. I-I have to go to-to the hospital later, and I already know if I let you touch me I won't be able to walk." There, I said it.

I knew what time it was. He and I both were well aware of what he wanted to do. He had the capability of pounding the attitude out of me or making me regret having an attitude to begin with.

"I'll take it easy on you, although that attitude you've been walking around here with has gotten on my last damn nerve. I should punish you, but I just want to feel my pussy. Now, come here." His head dropped back, and his stroke picked up.

Since I've known him, he's been demanding. When he called, he wanted me to answer regardless of what I was doing or who I was with. In college, when he wanted to see me or if I went against anything he demanded, he had no problem coming for me, and when he did, bless the heavens, the stars, and the moon! I paid for it. My pearl paid for it. The rules were simple; when I need you, answer or get tossed up…literally.

"Lilah, please baby," he moaned loudly.

Us women are known for our loudness in the bedroom. In our bedroom, Kellon was more vocal and unashamed about it. When we had guests over you'd think he'd be considerate. Absolutely not.

Without my permission, my hands removed his shirt that I wore. Removed the socks. Removed the boxer briefs. Rising on my knees, I moved closer to the edge of the bed where he stood. His head was still tossed back, and his hand movements had slowed down.

Without my permission, my head descended south, and my tongue outstretched from my mouth to catch the drip of his cream that coated his tip.

"Shit!" he bellowed.

His hands dropped away as I took over and reintroduced my lover to my tonsils. Sucking in my jaws, I licked and slurped until he stood on his tippy toes. His moans and praises only motivated me to get extra nasty.

"Damn, Lilah. Look at me." He wrapped my hair around his hand and pulled my head back.

When we first started having sex, I couldn't look him in the eye while I gave him head. I was too shy. I knew the minute that I gave in to his wish I'd come undone, and I did. The passion and hold he had on me was so intense that I released my own orgasm before him. One time was all it took for him to demand me to look him in the eyes and I've been hooked since. That eye to eye contact was no joke.

Not once did I break eye contact as I slurped and stroked him faster. A ripple of excitement hit me as his moans and words grew louder. When I began to hum and became lost in my own pleasure of pleasuring him, he gripped my hair tighter.

"Kellon," I yelped as he picked me up and tossed me on the bed. My giggles were short-lived as he smacked my engorged pearl with his swollen head. I couldn't deny the spark of excitement running through my veins at the prospect of knowing what was about to happen. My insides jangled with excitement.

"Damn, Lilah, I ain't even in you yet and you creaming the sheets. Mm, shit." He lowered his head, but I stopped him. The teasing and games were over. I wanted him inside me.

Wrapping my hand around his thick hardened shaft, I positioned him at my entrance. "Look at my pussy. She kissing all over my dick." The sound of his voice affected me intensely. Nothing turned me on more than hearing Kellon talk nasty to me.

"Kellon." I let out a combination of a hiss and a moan as he pushed deeper inside of me. My back arched off the bed. Toes curled. Hands griped the sheets. Eyes rolled into the back of my head. Kellon's love was painful.

Painfully good.

Connecting our hands together, he drew them up above my head and laid his chest against mine. "I love you, Delilah. I love everything about you. Do you still love me, Lilah?" His strokes were slow but long and meticulous. "Tell me you love me."

I couldn't speak. How could I when my voice was in my toes? I tried to release my hands from his grasp. He kept going deeper and harder. Driving me over the edge. Hitting places. New places. After being married for all these years, I thought he hit every spot within my walls. No. Each time he buried himself deep within, he found a new spot. And a new spot. And a new spot.

"Kellon," I moaned as tears hit my eyes. "Kellon..." I said his name over and over as he stroked me into oblivion.

"I'm trying to be fair, Lilah. You know if I shift it's over. Now tell me what I want to hear, baby. Tell me, baby. Tell me you love me. Tell me this my pussy. Tell me." Irresistible; his allure was so potent.

One of the places I wore my hearing aid continuously was the bedroom. I developed this obsession with hearing Kellon moan and express his pleasure in my ear. His hot breath tickling my ears. Then he'd do that weird kinky tongue thing where we exchanged saliva.

"It-It's yours, Kellon." He bit my neck, and I swear I saw stars. "I love you so much, Kellon. So much. Yes, baby. Don't stop." My heart hammered in my ears as I exploded.

Leaning back, he sat up on his knees and smirked at me. Grabbing my left leg, he turned me on my side and threw my leg over his shoulder. I hated this position. Hated it with so much passion. It was the position of submission for me. It provided the perfect angle for Kellon's curved dick to rub up against my g-spot.

"Nah, keep your hands to yourself." He pushed my hands away from his stomach. He was too deep. The pressure was too much. It all became too much.

"Please…" I begged as I stuffed my face in the pillows. Relentlessly he danced over my spot until I howled out. Not cry, but howl like a wild animal. "I'm…I'm…oh, my goodness…shit." I banged my fist against the bed.

"What's wrong, baby? You okay?" His humor died out as I squeezed my muscles around him. "Delilah!" His voice hit a high-pitched note as he spanked me on the booty. "Don't do that shit again."

I didn't listen. I squeezed and squeezed until his movements became drunk. When he pulled out my eyes popped open, and I gave him a mean glare.

"Fuck." He leaned against the window panting with his eyes closed.

With wobbly legs and all, I sat up and crossed my arms over my chest. "Seriously, Kellon?"

He didn't answer me. Instead, he walked back over to the bed and scooped me up. Once he placed my legs over the crook of his arm, I realized what he was doing. I tried to wiggle out his grip, but he held me firm.

"Kellon, no. Don't."

He ignored my pleas and latched onto my swollen nipples. All was forgotten when he did that. My nipples were the gateway to my undoing.

"Wrap around me, Lilah." He spoke low. The lust in his eyes caused my heart to pound in an erratic rhythm.

Doing as he said, I wrapped my limbs around his body as he hoisted me in the air and then lowered me down on his shaft. I buried my face in his neck to stifle my cries.

There, in the middle of our bedroom floor, he sexed me dumb. This time I was the dumb, stupid, ignorant person.

"Look at me," he demanded.

Lifting my head, I stared into the eyes of my husband. The man that loved each of my flaws. The man that worked tirelessly to make sure I had all my heart's desire. The man that poured out his love for me every day. The man that satisfied my every need.

"Forgive me, Lilah. Please forgive me." His vulnerability rocked my soul. I stared into his eyes with amazement. He was so powerful and strong but didn't care about showing his emotions.

I wanted to tell him that I long ago forgave him thirty strokes ago. Part of me felt like he knew that as well, but he wanted to hear me say it. With each stroke Kellon gave me, the brick around my heart dismantled. Kellon possessed that kind of love that was the perfect antidote to a broken heart, and that's what he did. He loved on me until I forgave.

"I forgive you, Kellon," I spoke against his lips.

"You still love me?" His eyes searched intently. I knew if I said the wrong thing I could break him.

"I'll never stop." I kissed any doubt he had away. I replaced the doubt and fear of losing me with the reassurance that he would always have me.

"Give me what I want, baby," he strained. I knew he was close to reaching his peak. "Open up for me."

I managed to open my mouth and stick out my tongue as his strokes quickened. Once we were connected and he saw our tongues locked together, he grunted and moaned. He swelled, and that vein rubbed up against my walls, offsetting the wave building in my stomach.

"Squeeze me, baby." He didn't have to ask me twice. He pumped, and I squeezed, taking us to a sexual planet of all highs that only our soul-stirring passionate love could reach.

KELLON

"From that stupid grin on your face, I take it you and baby girl made up?" Khiver asked as he reclined in the seat across from me. The day had finally come. We were on the plane heading to Dallas to get Kiser.

I ran a hand over my head and grinned. If only he knew. Less than four hours ago I had to pry my hands away from around her body. Specs of her flavor were still present on my tongue.

Clearing my throat, I answered him. "Yeah. She seduced me and finally let me have my way with her." I snorted at my own remark. Delilah didn't have to try to seduce me. She did so without even knowing.

"I'm happy things are working out for y'all. Why she didn't want to come?"

The excuse Lilah gave me for not wanting to come with me to Dallas was weak, but I understood her reasoning. "She said she wanted me and Kiser to bond alone before he met her. I get it, but then again I don't."

She and I had a long talk about Kiser and our new responsibility as parents. Instead of making these rules or false expectations, we both agreed to take it one day at a time. To relish in the moment and try our best to keep Kiser alive through the summer.

"Paige wanted to know how long we planned on staying in Dallas. The single with Drew drops at midnight. What you wanna do?"

The thought of being away from Delilah for any amount of time made my stomach hurt. "We're turning right around and coming back. You can head to Pappadeaux while I get Kiser. We leaving as soon as he says goodbye to his mama."

Khiver shook his head and laughed. "Bro, you got it bad, but I love it. You give the rest of us men out here hope that true love does exist. Maybe one day I'll settle down." I caught the flash of sadness in his eyes.

Khiver and I were the same when it came to wanting a family and giving our all to one woman. By the time I met Delilah, Khiver had his heart broken twice and wasn't interested in having it done a third time. The Cambridge men loved hard and unapologetically. Some women couldn't handle that, and instead of saying so, they would rather break us instead. At least that was the case for Khiver.

I was every definition of possessive, stingy, clingy, and selfish when it came to *my* Delilah. There wasn't a day that went by that God didn't receive my praise for the woman he created for me. Delilah accepted me, all of me. In the beginning, it took her a while to understand the levels and depths of my love. When she realized it was only for her and hers alone to have, she embraced me and reciprocated it back tenfold.

"Enough about the mushy stuff. The media has been quiet. You plan to drop the news first or let them find out whenever?" Khiver brought up another subject I'd been avoiding

Being famous had its pros and cons. One of the main cons that I despised was my privacy. The blogs and gossip sites could post whatever they wanted about me. Majority of their stories were bogus and so far from the truth. Paige did her best to keep her ears to the media and kept me informed on what had already been said. To be honest, I thought Sasha would have already leaked the information. She was or used to be scandalous like that.

I boldly flaunted Delilah on all my social media accountants. I had no plans on hiding Kiser.

When we landed, I called Delilah several times. Each call went straight to voicemail. I tried texting her, but my text stayed on 'delivered.' Delilah blocked me. I stressed myself to a migraine trying to figure out if I missed something before I left. She showed no signs of anger for her not to want to talk to me.

I got so lost in my thoughts and trying to calm myself down that I hadn't heard the driver tell me we had reached Sasha's house. She and her family lived in a nice sized two-story home that sat on acres of land. Bikes, balls, and other toys sprawled out in the yard.

As I approached the front door, I could hear kids horse playing around. My heart raced as I lifted my hand to knock. Meeting Kiser had me on edge. He and I talked on the phone all the time, but this was different. Our conversations were about his interest and my music. Not once did he question where I been all this time.

"Hey, Kellon." Sasha greeted with a little boy wrapped around her leg.

"Hey. What's up, little man." I held my fist out, and he gave me a fist bump.

"You're KC. I saw you on TV." He smiled revealing a toothless smile.

"Yeah, that was me. What's your name?"

Before he could answer, another little boy identical to him ran over and pushed in between Sasha's legs. "I'm Weiland. Are you Kiser's dad?"

"He asked me first." The little boy that was wrapped around Sasha's leg stood and pushed Weiland back. "My name is William Jr."

"Boys, go play. Come in, Kellon." Sasha stepped aside and let me pass. Will Jr. and Weiland stood back and eyed me with curiosity. "Do I need to repeat myself?" Hearing the threat in their mother's voice, they shook their heads and took off down the hall.

"Busy little boys," I said as I took in her home. I relaxed a little knowing that she didn't have my son living in nasty conditions.

"They are. Kiser is checking to make sure I packed everything he needed. You can follow me." I followed her to a larger living area with a mounted television and plush couches. Sitting in a recliner was a man that I assumed was her husband.

"Honey, this is Kellon. Kellon, this is my husband Will."

Will and I were around the same age, but Lupus caused him to look twice his age. Dark circles and bags hung under his eyes. His skin looked pale even though he was almost as dark as me. The clothes that he wore draped loosely off his body.

"Nice to meet you." He held his hand out for me to shake.

"Same here." I shook his hand and sat down on the couch opposite of him.

Sasha said Will was sick but seeing him in person he didn't appear that he was doing well at all. A wave of sadness came over me thinking of the gene test that was done on the boys. Little Will and Weiland appeared healthy but from the pictures on the wall, Will Sr. was once healthy also. It might sound cruel for me to say, but I'm glad Kiser wouldn't have to experience that.

To keep myself from staring at him, I looked around at the photos on the wall. Sitting in the awkward silence was becoming too much for me. "Where is Kiser?"

Sasha stood up and then sat back down. Kiser stood in the doorway eyeing me. Scratching my head, I stood and walked over to him. I noticed his height first. All the men in my family stood well over six feet. At eight years old he came to my stomach, surpassing his Mothers height. It wouldn't be long before he towered over Delilah.

Staring at the younger version of me felt like I was looking at a combination of Khiver and I. The Cambridge genes were strong, but... to see it... to see the life that I created... it was overwhelming.

Kiser inspected me the same as I had done him. I wanted to blame somebody for the years I missed out on. But there was no one else to blame. Sasha and I both were to blame. Neither of us was responsible adults when it came to the wellbeing of Kiser. She should've never tried to make him someone else's son, and I should've been adamant about finding out if he was mine or not.

"I'm ready." Hearing the raspy voice in person made my chest constrict.

I missed his first words. His first steps. And the fact that he has called another man daddy for the last eight years ticked me off.

"We're gone." I tossed over my shoulder but stopped once I reached the entryway. Walking over to Will, I held out my hand. "Tomorrow a doctor will call you. He's one of the best. There is no cost to you. It's the least I can do to thank you for raising my son as your own when you didn't have to."

The minute Will's face filled with emotions I released his hand and walked out the door. Kiser stood next to his mother as she took pictures of him and his brothers. I stepped to the side and called Delilah one more time. No answer. My patience was growing thin with the games she was playing.

"Kellon, you ready?" Kiser called from the back seat of the truck.

Walking over, I opened the door to get in but stopped when Sasha called my name. "Um, we're going to Tennessee in July for the fourth. If you and Kiser want to tag along let me know."

"I'll get with Delilah and let you know. We may already have plans. I have to check with her."

Her face scrunched up like she smelled a foul odor. "What does she have to do with anything?"

I tried to control my frustration. With Delilah not answering my calls and Sasha in my face with this bullshit, I was about to lose it.

"Kiser is with *me* for the summer. If my *wife* has plans or doesn't want to meet you and your *husband*, then no, it won't happen." I slammed the door in her face and instructed the driver to pull off.

Kiser and Khiver talked most of the ride to the airport while I sat back thinking of what was going through Delilah's mind. Before the plane took off, I called and called. None of the feelings I felt had me on edge to think something terrible happened to her, but I pulled up the security cameras from our house on my iPad to be sure.

She wasn't home, and from the activity chart, she left thirty minutes after I did. I rewound the camera footage to the exact moment she left. In her hands were bags. Not one bag but three bags.

She left me.

"Are you okay, Kellon?" Kiser's eyes were wide as he studied my face.

Remembering that this was the time for me to bond with my son, I stuffed my iPad in my bag and gave him my attention. "I'm good, Kiser."

I relaxed my posture and smiled. "Are you excited about spending the summer with me?"

He perked up in his seat with wide eyes. "Super excited. Do you have a pool? I want to go swimming." Seeing him so excited brightened my mood a little.

"Yes, we have a pool. Um," Scratching my head, I sucked up my pride and apologized. "I want to apologize for not being there for you all these years. I was immature." I expected Kiser's excited expression to lessen, but it grew.

"It's cool. My mom told me how she didn't tell you and that Will wasn't my real dad. Will is cool and treats me nice, but you're super cool." Khiver and I laughed at his energy.

"We'll be touching down soon. Are you hungry?" Khiver asked Kiser.

"Can we get some barbeque? I want some ribs with extra sauce." He rubbed his tummy and laughed.

"Little man is definitely your child." Khiver chuckled.

I sat back and watched Kiser talk with Khiver. I had a son. What if Will never got sick? Would Sasha have ever reached out to me?

DELILAH

What can I say? I'm a coward. I let my husband make love to me like it was the last time and then when he left for the airport I hightailed it out of there. My sudden disappearance stemmed from me not wanting to bring my unresolved issues into my new relationship with Kiser. Out of everyone involved, he was innocent. I knew my heart had hardened, and the last thing I ever wanted to do was take my frustrations and insecurities out on an innocent child.

Woody and I had a girl's trip already planned that kicked off three days after I landed, but I needed a quicker escape, so I came down to Jamaica early. This much-needed vacation gave me the perfect opportunity to think, cry, pray, yell out in anger, and cry.

I thought a lot over these last few days. Thought about whether or not I wanted to have Heather carry our child. Thought of Kiser, my marriage, and sadly, the possibility of me not ever being able to birth a child.

I needed this time away from my husband to think. Regardless of when Kiser was conceived, he was here, and I wanted to be cleansed to journey with my husband through his new adventure of fatherhood.

"I'm excited for you. I think you should do it." Woody said as she laid out next to me on the lounge chair. Neither of us needed a tan, but the sun felt good baking on our nude bodies. "What has Kellon said about it?"

Closing my eyes, I stretched and turned over. "To be honest, I haven't mentioned it to him. Ever since we got off the tour, we've been dealing with Sasha and Kiser. I'll tell him eventually."

During my alone time here, I thought about what was missing from my life. I had to understand why this situation affected me so. Yes, I was upset that my husband had an outside child, but it wasn't like Kiser was conceived during my marriage. I had long ago forgiven him for cheating with Sasha. Maybe if the news hadn't come right after I experienced such a traumatic miscarriage, it would have stung less.

Then there was the fact that I had this hidden layer of anger towards Kellon. I blamed him for snatching my dreams of becoming a nurse. Not once did he hold a gun to my head and tell me I couldn't. I chose not to because I wanted to be with him every second of the day. But still, I blamed him for my unhappiness.

Working in a hospital or doctor's office was out the question. Kellon and I traveled too much for that, and those jobs didn't offer a flexible schedule. While I've been here, thinking and praying, I decided to become a midwife. My love for babies and caring for pregnant mothers was a real passion of mine. Being nicknamed the baby whisperer wasn't given to me for nothing. I had a gift, and I wanted to share my gift.

I wanted to deliver the babies that I couldn't have. Maybe this was deeper than a passion, but my purpose. To pour my hurt into bringing life into the world. Maybe the babies weren't supposed to come from my womb, but me helping bring the babies to life from their mother's womb.

"If I could, I would walk around naked all the time, after I get a breast reduction though. These big shits hurt after a long day at work." Woody groaned.

"Williamenia August, you and I both know Carter is not going for that." I giggled as she sat up and shot me an evil glare.

"Carter has no say so when it comes to my body. Well, other than in the bedroom, but that's it." The blaring of a ringing phone paused our conversation. "It's not right to ignore him like this, Lilah. I get it but at least put the man out of his misery by letting him hear your voice, and not hear it on your voicemail."

Snatching up my kimono, I stood. "Fine. I'll be back."

With each step I took my stomach dropped. He wasn't calling. He facetimed me. A total of six days since I've seen his milk chocolate face. Swiping my finger across the screen, I waited for his face to come in clear. I swallowed the large lump in my throat as he stared back at me. He didn't give me his usual natural snarl. What I got was a look of relief and sadness that caused me to feel guilty.

"When are you coming home?" The desperation in his voice caused my shoulders to slump. What had I done? I never meant to hurt him.

"Tomorrow…our plane lands tomorrow night." I bit the inside of my cheek in hopes to mask my need of wanting to reach out to him. I knew this would happen. There was no resisting Kellon Cambridge. I craved him too much.

"Are you naked right now?" The pitch in his baritone changed to a tone of anger and disbelief.

I clamped my eyes shut and cursed under my breath. I forgot to tie the kimono when I walked inside the house. The beach house that Woody and I were staying at sat sectioned off in a private area. No one came here. We didn't even have staff. It was just her and I.

"Uh ye-yeah. We-We were sitting out by the pool." I felt like a child that got caught doing something they weren't supposed to be doing. Well, in a sense I was. I was walking around naked without a care to the world knowing that all it took was for one peeping tom to look over the large privacy fence and recognize my face.

"Are you enjoying yourself?" He spoke calmly, but the anguish hid in the background.

Nodding, I smiled. "I am. How is Kiser?"

"I don't want to talk about him right now." That same large lump came back up and lodged itself in the middle of my throat making it hard for me to breathe. "You still love me, Delilah?"

Closing my eyes, I thought back to the last time he made love to me. My body trembled. I still felt him inside of me even though he hadn't touched me in days. "I love you more than you know."

"Look at me, baby." He commanded me. I shook my head. The levy was breaking. I had to stand firm to keep the guard up. "Delilah Mari, you are my world, mama. The ache I feel in my chest is becoming unbearable. The magnitude of my love for you scares me. I'm not afraid to admit that you scare me. You took my life supply of air. I've had to endure six sleepless nights without my air to breathe. Come home to me, Lilah, so I can breathe."

My cheeks were drenched. I felt his pain. I hadn't been able to breathe since I walked out our home. "I'll come home." I opened my eyes and stared into his red eyes. Wiping away the tears, I smiled. "Tell me about Kiser."

Stretching, I smiled as the sun beat down on my face. Sleeping with the windows and balcony doors open allowed the wind to breeze through my room and provide some of the best sleep I've had in months. Jamaica owed me nothing. It gave me what I needed. A place of refuge and cleansing.

Turning over, I screamed at the top of lungs. Scooting back from being startled, I fell out the bed and landed on the cold wood floors. "Damnit, Kellon," I screeched as I hopped up holding my chest. He laid there staring at me saying nothing, but his eyes said plenty.

Reaching for my kimono, I wrapped it around my body and crossed my arms across my chest. "What are you doing here?"

Moving the sheets to the side, he stood up revealing that he had on grey sweats with no shirt. "You sleep too hard, Lilah. I don't like that I came into your room and laid next to you without you budging." He frowned as he put his shirt on and slid his feet in his slides.

My mouth watered as I took him in. He scared the shit out of me, but he did so looking edible. Clearing my throat, I repeated myself. "Why are you here?"

He sat down on the edge of the bed and chuckled. "Yo, you ain't in no position to question me about anything. Put some clothes on so we can go." He nodded his head towards the sweat suit and shoes laid out on the dresser.

Looking around the room, I noticed my bags were packed by the door. I opened my mouth to speak, but he shut me up with the look on his face. I knew he was pissed. The fact that he came to Jamaica two days after I promised I would be home proved it.

"Woody is gone already." He stood and walked past me to the balcony. "You out here living your best life while I'm home trying to bond with my son, but I can't because I'm worried about you. I don't appreciate the shit you pulled, Lilah. Let this be the last time you pull a stunt like this."

I nodded even though his back faced me. Putting on my clothes, I made sure to watch him. He would never hurt me. That I knew. But seeing him like this, scared me. I crossed the line.

Walking into the bathroom, I noticed all my toiletries were packed as well. The only thing on the counter was my travel toothbrush and toothpaste. I brushed my teeth and fixed my hair in record timing. When I walked back out, he wasn't in the room nor were my bags. Diego and X were standing by the front door as I walked down the stairs.

"Hey, Mrs. D, you ready?" Not sure what to say, I nodded and followed them out the door.

Getting inside the sprinter, my throat became dry. Kellon sat watching me with so much disappointment. Taking a seat next to him, I reached up behind my ear to grab my hearing aid. His strong hand wrapped around my wrist stopping me.

"Don't you dare," he seethed.

Lord forgive me. I know this is a serious matter but got damnit if that didn't just have me leaking.

His security made sure we were straight before pulling off and headed towards the airport. Kellon turned towards me with my wrist in his grasp. I watched as he bit the corner of his mouth and his forehead wrinkled.

"My son, whom I just met, is staying over my parents' house while I hopped my black ass on a plane to get you." I opened my mouth to correct him. Nobody told him to do any of that. "And if you fix your mouth to say ain't nobody told me to leave him I will fuck you up." I gulped at his brass tone.

"You wanted a girl's weekend. Cool. Fine. I spared no expenses. But the fuck shits you pulled by being here for a damn week is unacceptable, Delilah. What the fuck, man?" He shoved my wrist out his grasp and pinched the bridge of his nose. I sat on my hands trying to hide the trembles rolling through my body.

"I'm a grown ass man, Delilah. When you needed me, I stepped in and became your leverage as you dealt with the miscarriages. I sucked up my feelings and placed yours in the forefront because you're my woman. That's my job. I needed you there with me when I went to get Kiser. Instead of being by my side you gave me some sorry ass excuse. I took that L and kept it moving. Then, here I am thinking that when we get home, you'll be there to help me get him adjusted to spending his first night in our home.

You're the child expert. I know nothing about fucking kids, but I was excited to try because my wife knows it all." He chuckled and flicked his nose. "Jokes on me when I step foot in my house and that shit empty and feels like less of a home. Imagine my surprise and Kiser's."

"I'm sorry," I mumbled wiping tears from my eyes.

"My feelings are hurt, Lilah. The same way I'm there for you is the way I expected you to be there for me. Kiser may not have your blood, but he has mine which makes him a part of you. He's *our* son." Kellon wrapped his arm around my waist and placed me on his lap.

"This discord in our communication stops right here. Your feelings. Your business. Your emotions. You period is my business and vice versa." He used the back of his hand to wipe my tears away. "I'm pissed as hell right now. I shouldn't have had to come and get you and make you come home."

"Kellon, I'm sorry. I-I…" he shushed me with his lips.

"Nah, I don't want to hear it. Got me out here acting a complete fool. Talking to you all rough and shit." He sprinkled kisses along my jaw and neck. Giggling, I shoved his head away. "And you better not tell my daddy either." Gripping my chin between his fingers, he turned my face towards him. "When we get back home, don't step foot in that house with the shits. What's done is done. I said what I said, and we are moving on. You understand?"

I was a sick individual. How was I torn between sucking the soul out his dick or wanting to climb his bones?

"Yes, daddy," I purred.

Chuckling, he kissed me one last time and released my chin. "Now lay your ass down and get some sleep. You in time out." He placed my head on his chest. As best as I could, I wrapped myself in his arms and did as I was told.

KELLON

"Grandma, these don't taste like the batch we made the other day. What you did differently?" Kiser spit out the chocolate cookies and side-eyed my mother.

Pops, Khiver, and I stood to the side snickering. Cassandra Cambridge prided herself on being a connoisseur in the kitchen. She baked better than any bakery in town. Fried the best fish in the south. To see my son spit out her signature chocolate chip cookies and then question her recipe was a priceless moment.

"Blame it on your ugly granddaddy. I told him I needed salt. Hardhead makes an upset stomach. Here, try these red velvet cupcakes." She pushed a cupcake into his face only for him to jump back.

"No, ma'am. If you didn't put salt in the cookies, then I know you didn't put any in the cupcakes." Kiser shook his head as he walked out of the kitchen.

"Don't y'all just stand there. The nerve of these new generation children." My Mother tossed the dish towel on the counter and frowned at my Father. "You had one job, Bishop. One job." She kissed her teeth and pointed at Khiver. "Go to the store and take your father with you. Show him what salt looks like since he can't seem to tell the difference between salt and baking soda."

"Ruby, don't act like that." Pops moved to touch her, but she gave him a glare that stopped him in his tracks. "Fine, come on, boy."

I waited until I heard the front door close before I pushed off the wall and sat on the stool across from the counter. After dropping Delilah off at the house, I headed straight to my parent's house. I knew she wanted to come but her time out wasn't over yet.

"What's on your mind, pretty lady? Kiser ain't give you no problems, did he?"

She held her frown for another minute until her lips curved up into a smile. "Fatherhood looks good on you. I'm proud of you for stepping up, and no. He and your Father stayed up longer than I could hang last night."

"I guess. That's good though. Thank you again." The praises that people gave me left a sour taste in my mouth. I would never neglect my child. I may have been irresponsible about how I handled everything in the beginning. Being a deadbeat wasn't in my DNA.

"I miss my baby girl. How long you plan on making her suffer?" She drummed her fingers on the countertop. She asked the question I've wanted to know myself.

"That has yet to be determined. Ma, keep it real with me. You think I love Delilah too much?" Nothing I came up with could explain why she left for a week. For seven whole days, she strutted around Jamaica like she lost her damn mind and lied about when she was coming home. Had I not gone and got her myself ain't no telling when she would've came home. I needed direction because whatever I caused to make her act out this way, I had to make sure I didn't do it again.

With amusement in her eyes, she snorted. "Answer your own question, Kellon. Do you think you love her too much?"

Shrugging my shoulders, I answered honestly. "I don't think I love her enough."

She paused washing the plate in her hand and turned towards me with wide eyes. "Explain this to me, son. I see the love you give Delilah. It surpasses the love your Father gives me. Has she said that you don't love her enough?" That quickly she went from defending her daughter-in-law to protecting me.

"That's how I feel. What else can be the reason for her to leave like that? I knew about the girl's trip with Woody. I paid for the shit. But she left me, Ma. That trip was only for three days. It's been a week. She couldn't face me and tell me to my face that she needed space to breathe." I banged my fist on the counter as my eyes watered.

I hated being in my feelings. These last few days I found myself depressed with no appetite. Worrying and stressing. Had me ready to paint the city red just to relieve some stress. Delilah forced my hand. I had to revert back to the old Kellon and snatch her ass from Jamaica. There wasn't too much in the world that bothered me, but when it came to my feelings and my wife, I quickly stepped back into my old ways, and there was no such thing as controlling me.

"Baby, answer me this. Have you taken time to heal from those miscarriages? Have you dealt with losing three children?"

My words weren't needed to answer her question. The hot tears running down my face responded for me.

Rushing to my side, she wrapped her arms around me and hugged me. "Oh, Kellon."

"Ma," I choked on my tears. "Nobody knows how reckless I was living in the streets. I was living foul, Ma. I did some grimy shit. I used to fear the conversation I'd have with God when I had to answer for my sins, but that changed when He gave me the greatest gift on this earth. I knew then that I could stand in front of Him and be held accountable for my past because of my present, the man I am now," I shook my head and wiped my face.

"If I never got anything right, I know for a fact that I loved His daughter, the woman He created for me. Do you know how hard it is for me to remain strong when my wife is crumbling to pieces in my hands? How hard was it to push my feelings to the side to be there for her? She's innocent, Ma. My baby is sweet with a heart of gold, so why is God punishing her for my sins?

She asked me over and over to tell her how I felt about losing the babies, but I lied each time. I had to be strong for her. For us." Standing, I looked towards the room Kiser sat in. "Seeing him...I'll never get that with my wife."

73

"Kellon, you don't know that. Don't give up on trying, baby. I know it's hard but don't stop trying." She wiped my tears and kissed my cheek. "Son, I can't tell you why you guys are going through all this, but what I will say is never stop loving her the way you do. I can't imagine how she would've pushed through had you stopped."

I took in what my Mother said and tried to see the bigger picture. Tried to place myself in Delilah's shoes and feel what she was feeling. A weight lifted off my shoulders the more I talked with my Mother. I'd been carrying that baggage for years. Delilah wasn't the only one who was hurt or traumatized after dealing with losing our kids. As a man, my duty was to be her strength, and that's what I did.

"**B**oy, you heavy as hell," I grunted with each step I took going up the stairs. "You complained about grandma cookies, but you ate something to make your ass so damn heavy." Laying Kiser on the bed, I removed his shoes and tucked him under the covers. The kid barely moved and not once did his manly snores stop.

My eyes fluttered from the flowery smell creeping into the room. She glided across the wood floor until she stood over Kiser's bed. Running a hand over his head, she smiled and leaned down. "You're so beautiful." She kissed his cheek and walked out like I wasn't standing right here.

Taking my time, I locked up the house. The half-empty bottle of Hennessy stared back at me as I sat at the kitchen table drinking my second glass. Seeing her after all this time did something to me. It awakened this unruly hunger. I know I said she had to sit in time out, but I had other things in mind to make her pay for playing with me.

Grabbing my glass of liquor, I headed upstairs. She probably wanted to talk. Nah, the talking could wait until morning. The only thing I wanted to hear was her begging me to stop. She had to pay for what she did. I wasn't a man that sat in his feelings. Then on top of that, she left me for a week. A damn week. After nine years together, you'd think she realized that I was selfish.

She was mine.

All mine.

It was my ring she wore. My last name she carried. My smell on her. My name is written on the walls of her pussy.

It's cool. Tonight, I'd just have to remind her. Kiser being a heavy sleeper worked in my favor. I'd hate to traumatize him by seeing Delilah for the first time in a figure four.

"Are...are you drinking Hennessey?" Her voice was fragile and shaky as she peered up at me with scared eyes.

With my eyes trained on her, I emptied the glass in one gulp. Her eyes began widening as I removed my shirt. Kneeling beside the tub, I grabbed her loofah and squeezed a large amount of her body wash on it. The panicky stare she watched me with only grew my craving.

Her lips parted. Before she could speak, I placed a finger over lips and shook my head. She opened her mouth to speak again. This time I kissed her words away. Multitasking, I washed her body and reacquainted myself with her lips. I pressed a gentle kiss against hers, then tenderly covered her mouth with mine. I wanted to suck her lips off her face.

When her moans grew louder, I pulled back. I laughed at the frown and pout she gave me. "Fix your face." Taking her hands in mine, I helped her out and into the shower to rinse off. Each time she tried to speak I sucked the words out her mouth. Eventually, she stopped trying to talk once her lips became swollen and red.

Her brandy eyes fought to stay open. The feel of the warm oil and my hands rubbing over her body spellbound her into an ecstasy haze. I know she wanted to touch me. Talk to me. Delilah knew the calming, meditating, unwinding of my day occurred when I prepared her for bed.

It started with the tension in my shoulders releasing when I bathed her. The stress of business relieved as I rubbed her down in her favorite body butter or oils. Lyrics to some of my biggest hits came from massaging her scalp. My thoughts become clear and my mind less foggy after I tucked her in bed. Although tonight, no one would get tucked in...yet.

Her body was my playground, and I wanted to play.

"Kellon," She moaned from the pressure I applied to the spot behind her knees.

Delilah had this all wrong. Me pleasing her. Rubbing her down. This wasn't for her pleasure. This was for my own. It just so happened that my pleasure came from pleasing her. She lucked out either way.

My lips kissed various spots on her body. I had to make sure I wasn't hallucinating or dreaming. My air to breathe was home.

"Kellon," Her moans were driving me crazy. Only she could say my name like that.

"Yes, baby," I answered as I hovered over her well that never ran dry for me. A whiff wouldn't do it. I needed access to the full meal.

"Let's g-go to bed. You had too much to drink." She tried to push my head away. I hadn't even touched her yet, and already she was running.

Standing, I removed the rest of my clothes. Her eyes were in slits from the high I placed her in just from the feel of my hands. "You know what I drank, right?" She nodded and purred. Her legs squeezed together as her hands squeezed her breast. "I'm giving you the option to pick first. You can either sit on my face or let me have my way. It's up to you." My hand ran over the tattoo of her name on my chest as I watched her squirm and moan on the bed.

Unsure of whether to grip the sheets or the bed, she began to whine. "Kellon, please, let's just sleep. Let the Henny wear off."

Chuckling, I walked over to my nightstand. "Hardhead makes a sore pussy. I gave you the opportunity to choose how you were going to get this Henny dick." Reaching inside the drawer, I pulled out four black silk ropes.

Her eyes flew open when she felt the fabric on her ankle. "N-No, Kellon. No baby. I-I-I...let me choose again." She tried to run, but I grabbed her ankle and tied it to the bed post. When I reached for her other ankle, she moved it out of my reach.

Titling my head, I smirked. "Lilah, baby, you know I will tie that leg to the headboard. That pussy will be wide open. You got one second to dec– good girl." She dropped her leg down before I could finish. When I reached her hands, her body was shaking like she was seizing. "Do I need to turn the music on?" She didn't answer me. Her eyes were stuck staring at my dick that had swelled to the point it became painful.

Knowing what I was about to do to her, I turned the music on. Kiser slept hard, but no one could sleep through the screams of Delilah when I took her like this.

"I missed you, Lilah," I spoke against her skin as I laid flat on the bed between her legs. Using my thumbs, I spread her glistening lips apart and blew on her clit causing her to arch her upper body off the bed. "You miss me, baby?" I spoke to both sets of lips.

"Keeellllloooonnnnn." Her purr was music to my ears.

Popping her gently on her clit, I watched as her legs shook. "Mmm, you taste good." Coating my tongue with her nectar, I became angry all over again. How dare she deprive me of my pussy for seven whole days because she was in her feelings? And the nerve of her to walk around naked like it wasn't my shit that she was flaunting around?

The more I thought about the pain she caused me by leaving, the more selfish I became as I relentlessly feasted. Her pleas were drowned out by the music. The violent shakes of her body were ignored. All that mattered was making the next orgasm bigger and better than the one before.

I wasn't a selfish lover by far. Three orgasms were the minimum when I feasted. Now when I wanted to be greedy, I didn't stop until there were tears and she blacked out.

It wasn't until I met Delilah, tasted both sets of lips, that I found out I had a jealous streak. There was no sharing.

Wiping a hand over my beard and glancing down at my chest, I chuckled. Her nectar showers were the best.

Kissing up her body, she flinched wherever my lips touched. Her skin had become sensitive to the point she whimpered with tears threatening to fall.

"Try and leave me again, Delilah, and I promise I'll suck you until you lose brain activity. Try me." I glared into her eyes. "You love me?" Positioning myself at her drenched opening, I waited for her answer before I made us one.

Straining against the ropes, she nodded her head. "So much, Kellon. I

uch." Leaning down, I licked her tears and kissed her lips.
n," she moaned in my mouth as I plunged into her in one

dropped my head in her neck and took a deep breath. If I moved, it would be over.

Being inside of her was better than anything I ever felt. She curved to me. Curved and suctioned me with those walls with my name on it. Healed and restored me. Our chemistry couldn't be measured. My infatuation started with how she loved me but grew when she submitted to me.

The way her body spoke to me, asking and begging me to go harder. Go slower. Go deeper. My territorial behavior ignited at the sound of my name drumming from her lips.

"I wanna touch you, Kellon. Please release me." I shook my head. The minute she'd touch me it would be over. I had to have this control. "Let me feel you."

Rising on my knees not breaking our connect, I pushed her legs wider. "You can't feel me, Lilah?" Gripping her thighs, I leaned down just a little and hammered into her.

Her screams bounced off the walls. I bit down on my lip to keep my need to join in. Her tiny hands clenched and unclenched into a fist. Her head thrashed back and forth. Her stomach tightened. It was coming.

"Repeat that for me," I gritted as I mercilessly dug until I touched the bottom of her pussy. Her walls closed in on me. Eyes rolled to the back of her head. Mouth hung open. "Say it again."

"I'm sorry," she cried out. The tears didn't move me. "Baby, it's too much. Too much. Shit...shit...shit...yessss." Not one to waste a meal, I moved down just in time to catch her essence. "Nooo...nooo. Kellon... you have to stop," she begged through her tears.

Knowing she couldn't move from being paralyzed by my loving, I untied her arms and legs. I laughed as she cupped her sex and turned on her side. I arched my brow. She must've known what she did immediately.

"No, Kellon. I-I...give...nooooo." Ignoring her pleas, I lifted her leg and tossed it over my shoulder. Leaning down and placing my fist near her head, I stroked her slower this time. Taking my time to hit every crevice. Making her cream and moan.

"I love you, Delilah Mari. There is no me without you," I whispered in her ear. Latching my lips onto her neck, I sucked until my mark was left.

"I love you too." She wrapped her arms around my neck and kissed me. "Give me what I want, Kellon." She stuck her tongue out. I groaned as I felt my nuts tighten and toes tingle. She knew how much I loved swapping spit. Leaning down, I sucked her tongue in my mouth and sped up. Reaching for her hands, I held them above her head as I released my seeds.

Our chests heaved up and down as we tried to catch our breath. The sweat and fluids needed to be washed off, but neither of us decided to move. Rolling over, not removing myself from her body, I held on to her until she laid comfortably on my chest. Reaching over, I grabbed the remote and turned the music off.

"Kellon, I'm sorry," she mumbled through her tiredness.

"I'm sorry too. I meant it when I said we'd have a big problem if you tried to pull another stunt like that. Let that be the last time you run off. Whether you realize it or not, everything I do, or you do, is *our* business. Now go to sleep. I'm tired." I reached for the covers and covered us.

She giggled and snuggled up until she got to her favorite place. The crook of my neck. "You so bossy. Why you had to punish me with the Henny dick? I won't be able to move for days, Kellon," she whined and bit my neck.

"Alright now. I still got one more round in me. Bite me again and you gon' be bedridden for the rest of the month."

"I can't even do it. Feeling you like this is enough. I hope Kiser didn't hear us." She raised her head and looked at me with worry.

Chuckling, I laid her head back down. "Don't worry. That kid sleeps hard as hell. Even if he did, he's with us for the summer. He would've eventually caught on to the fact that his daddy has no manners."

"Oh my gosh." She giggled. "I can't wait to meet him."

"He's a good kid, Lilah." I reassured her that she had nothing to worry about. He was just as excited to meet her.

of you so of course he is. Now stop talking. I'm sleepy."

mama."

, goodnight, baby."

DELILAH

I wonder if this is what falling in love, at first sight, felt like? Since I was a little girl, I've been a hopeless romantic, but believing in love, at first sight, was farfetched to me. This type of love was different. It wasn't love between a woman and a man, but a love between a mother and child. Standing in the middle of my kitchen, I felt my heart soften to mush. The hardened shell or what was left had fallen off. Looking into the tender young eyes of this child weakened me. It didn't matter that another woman carried him for nine months. It didn't matter that it wasn't my breast he nursed from.

All that mattered at this moment was Kiser.

Sometime during the middle of the night, Kellon carried us to the bathroom and bathed the residue of our reunion off our tired bodies. I barely moved. In my incoherent state, nothing registered. He washed me from head to toe and not once did I wake. The sheets on our bed were changed while he sat me in a chair. Nothing interrupted my sleep.

Waking before he did surprised me. Kellon rose hours before I did. However, this morning, after he rocked my world, I awoke with a need to prepare breakfast for my family. Not my husband, but my family.

The final biscuit had been buttered when I felt a presence enter the kitchen. The pitter patter of my heartbeat told me it wasn't Kellon. This song was different. I felt different. When I turned and looked into the smiling face of the younger version of my husband, I understood.

That quickly, Kiser thawed my heart just by his presence alone. He hadn't uttered a word, but I loved him. Staring into those familiar coal eyes, I fell in love as if I birthed him.

"You must be Delilah. I'm Kiser." He outstretched his long arm.

Giggling, I wiped my eyes before taking that arm into my hand and pulling him in for a hug. "Hi, Kiser. I'm so happy to meet you." I kissed his forehead and released him. "Are you hungry? Your Father has a large appetite. Do you eat any of this?" I waved a hand over the feast of breakfast food.

Plates of biscuits, eggs, bacon, corn beef hash, grits, and fruit covered my counters. His eyes bounced around, going from one plate to the next.

"I do. Can I have everything please?"

"Sure. Fix your drink, and I'll make your plate."

"Yes, ma'am." Gosh, could he be any more perfect?

I placed his plate in front of him and started cleaning up the kitchen. Having a messy kitchen irked my nerves. I couldn't eat with dishes all over the place.

The kitchen became too quiet. I expected to hear silverware scraping against the plate, but I heard nothing. Turning around, I noticed Kiser hadn't touched his plate. "You okay? Why haven't you touched your food?"

He smiled. "I'm waiting on you, Mrs. Delilah."

Am I a punk for wanting to cry? This little boy stole my heart. There was no denying it. He had me already wrapped around his finger. Then he had the nerve to have manners like his father.

Drying off my hands, I grabbed my plate and sat next to him. "Sorry about that." I went to bow my head to say my grace, but he stopped me.

Holding his hand out, he asked to lead. "Can I have your hand?" I placed my hand in his and bowed my head. "Dear God, thank you another day. Thank you for waking us up healthy and happy. Thank you for my family. Please bless this food for the nourishment of our bodies. In Jesus name, we pray, amen."

"Amen." I cleared my throat and turned my head before he could see my misty eyes.

The clinking of our forks touching the plates brought a smile to my face. He and I would steal glances at one another causing us to laugh.

"Kellon told me you decorated my room. I love it. Thank you." He patted my shoulder.

I wiped my mouth and smiled. "You're welcome. My best friend is the one who decorated it. I'll tell her you like it."

"How y'all gon' eat without me?" Kellon's deep voice entered the kitchen before he did.

I'm almost choked on my juice as he entered the kitchen. Shoulda known he wouldn't change who he was with his child around. He stood by the counter in nothing but boxer briefs and black socks. Nothing on Kellon's body was small. Nothing. Everything and I mean everything, was on display.

He smirked catching me ogle at his package. "Morning, family."

"Morning, Kellon." Kiser held out his fist.

"What's up, little man? How you sleep? Woke up during the middle of the night? Heard screaming?" Kellon winked at me as I ran a hand down the front of my neck.

I wanted to hide. Kiser shook his head causing me to release the breath I held onto for dear life. "No, sir. I slept good."

Changing the subject, I got up to make his plate. "What all do you want?"

"I got it. Sit down. I know you're sore." He bit down on his lip as he took my plate. After piling on more food to my plate, he came over and stood between Kiser and I. "Raise up." I pointed to the chair on the other side of Kiser hoping he'd get the hint. Sucking his teeth, he placed the plate on the table and scooped me up. "Ain't nothing changing 'cause he here. You already know what time it is. We ain't switching up." He positioned me on his lap until I sat sideways on his lap in Indian style.

My face reddened with embarrassment. He scooped up a spoonful of grits. "Open up, Mama." I glanced at Kiser who watched smiling and shook my head. "Mama, stop acting shy. Open up for me and let me feed you." There were so many hidden messages within that sentence.

"Kellon! Stop! He doesn't need to see us like this." I gritted avoiding Kiser's amused look.

"Man, what you mean?" I couldn't help but laugh. Kellon looked like someone stole his candy.

"Kellon, stop." I tried to get off his lap, but he used his free hand to grip around my waist.

"Aye, Kiser, is it bothering you that Delilah is sitting on my lap and I'm trying to feed her?" He leaned in and kissed my neck.

Okay, so Kellon and I had a few more weird lover's quirks. He loved for me to sit on his lap while we ate from the same plate. This all started when I would eat from his plate and not my own. So, to be able to cop a feel and stop me from fixing two unnecessary plates, we compromised on mixing it all together.

"Nope. We all gotta eat someway." Kiser shrugged his shoulders and turned his attention back to his plate.

"Let me warn you now. I'm very touchy with Delilah, she too juicy and sweet for me not to. You may see me smack her ass, slob her down, pop her ti–"

I placed a hand over his mouth. He threw his head back and laughed. "Kiser, baby, don't listen to your Father."

"Okay. Okay." He kissed my cheek. "Just for the safety of your eyes, turn your head when you see her and me in the same room." Thrusting his hips up he gripped the back of my neck and whispered in my ear. "You better be glad he sitting right here. I ain't done with you. We still got six days to make up for."

To avoid moaning, I spoke to Kiser. "What would you like to do today?"

Kiser raised his head from his plate and tapped his chin. "Well, what are you doing today, Delilah?"

"I'm going to the hospital to love on some newborn babies." For the first time in months, I got excited about rocking the newborns. I still haven't mentioned becoming a midwife to Kellon yet. We had a lot to talk about, but I knew it would have to be tabled with Kiser around.

"Can I go with you?"

I stopped mid-chew and looked at Kellon then Kiser. "Uh, that's fine. Are you sure though? We'll be around babies for about five hours."

"Yes, ma'am, I'm sure. I want to hang with you for the first part of my day and then with Kellon. If that's okay?" His response surprised both Kellon and me.

"Perfect. Eat up. We have to be leaving within the next thirty minutes. Babe, I'm about to get ready." I kissed Kellon and went upstairs.

Hearing Kiser say that he wanted to hang with me for the day tugged on my heartstrings. He tried to get to know me. That meant a lot. I felt guilty for staying away so long. Here I was thinking that he wouldn't accept me or feel I was trying to replace him Mom, but all he wanted to do was spend time with me.

"He's smitten with you." Kellon startled me.

Turning around, I grinned. "Are you jealous?"

Sitting down on the edge of the bed, he pulled me between his legs. "Not yet." Lifting his head, he gave me an intense gaze. "Are you mine, Lilah? Are you going to run from me again?"

I hated the position I placed him in. The position of being vulnerable and uncertain of where he stood in my life. It's crazy how the eyes can tell the hearts' truth, and his honesty was fear of our future. Cuffing his face in my hands, I touched his forehead with mine. "I will never leave you like that again, Kellon. It was selfish of me to not think about your feelings. Forgive me, baby?"

Placing his hands behind my knees, he pulled forward until I straddled his lap. "Talk to me, Mama. What can I do to make you happy?"

My face scrunched up. "I am happy, Kellon. Me leaving wasn't because you made me unhappy. I left because I had to get my feelings in order. I didn't want to bring my negative energy here with Kiser."

I could tell he wanted to push on, but he changed the subject. "You cool with him hanging with you at the hospital? I can take him to the studio with me."

Seeing him in a cool relaxed mood, I decided to share the news about my career change. To make sure that he stayed neutral with his thoughts and demeanor, I kissed along his jaw and neck. "Babe, I'm going to complete the certification process to become a midwife. What do you think?"

His hands roamed back and forth over my thighs. Placing his lips over mine, he murmured, "It's about time. I'm excited for you. Now, what about Heather's offer?"

Just like that my mood changed. Call me crazy or what have you, but my spirit hadn't settled on that matter. It wasn't that I didn't trust Heather to remain healthy while she carried our child. In the pit of my stomach laid a tiny grape seed of hope. Of faith that maybe God would bless us just once. The baby didn't have to come today or next month, but soon enough when He thought we were ready.

"Can we table that for another day?" I pleaded.

"Sure, now kiss me before he busts in here and catches me being mannish."

***

"Why is he shaking like that?" Kiser's big brown eyes widened as he studied the baby in the incubator.

"His body is suffering from withdrawals. While in the womb, he became addicted to heroin because of his mother." My lips trembled staring at the four-pound baby boy.

"That woman back there crying, is that his Mother?" He glanced over his shoulder for a moment and then turned back to the baby.

"Yes. Let's go. I have one more stop to make before we leave." There was only so much strength one could hold onto to not cry. This part of my job was the hardest. I never discriminated. A child in need was a child in need. No matter the circumstances, I'd hug them, rock them, hold their tiny hand, and feed them.

"Delilah, will that baby die?" Kiser asked with his head down.

Grabbing his hand, I gave a promising smile. "No, sweetie. He's a fighter. He'll make it through."

"That's good. Where are we going when we leave here?" He skipped alongside me as we headed towards human resources.

"It's up to you, bud. I can take you to your Father or do something.

You tell me." Glancing over the papers in my hand, I said a quick prayer and then laid them on the desk.

All of the required paperwork needed to get started on becoming a midwife was in that folder. The process would begin once they accepted my application. I hadn't felt this eager to start a new journey in a while.

"How about ice cream?"

Pulling out my car keys I nodded. "Sure. I'll take you to my favorite ice cream place. Race you to the car." Like a kid, I took off running with him chasing behind me.

When we arrived at Jaxson's, Kiser's eyes lit up. The old nostalgia ice cream factory made the best homemade ice cream in the world. People traveled near and far to taste the history of Jaxson's. Food Network had listed it as one of Florida's top hidden treasures. Since then, the lines stayed wrapped around the building. When Kellon and I had a date night, we would come early before the crowd got too long or opted for takeout.

"Are you sure you can eat all of that?" I smirked at Kiser who tried with all his might to eat the large four scoop ice cream cone.

Like a typical Saturday night, the lines were wrapped around the building. The takeout line hadn't reached the parking lot yet when we arrived. Kiser made my day by saying he didn't want to wait in the line for inside dining. We stood in line for about ten minutes before we reached the front of the line and ordered enough ice cream to feed a small village.

"Oh yes. I can," he cheered.

Giggling at the faces he made, I took my phone out and snapped a few pictures. "Come on, kid. Your father is waiting." All of the extra pounds of ice cream I ordered were for Kellon, Khiver, and whoever else was in the studio. Kellon would have a fit if he knew I went to Jaxson's and didn't bring him back anything.

"Thank you for letting me hang with you, Delilah. I had fun." Kiser surprised me by wrapping his lanky arms around my waist.

Kissing the top of his, I hugged him back. "The pleasure was all mine. Thank you."

Hand in hand, we walked into Strong Arm studios. Kellon must've let it be known that Kiser was coming. The usual stench of weed and liquor weren't polluting the air. We headed up to the second floor were Kellon recorded. Khiver and the AR guy were sitting around talking. A few other guys were there that I didn't know.

"Uncle Khi." Kiser released my hand and ran over to Khiver.

"What's going on, little man? Hey, Lilah." He kissed my check and eyed the bag in my hand. "Is that what I think it is?"

"And it's not for you," Kellon spoke from behind me. "Hey, Mama." Kissing my cheek, he gripped my hips. "How was he?"

Handing him the bag of ice cream, I stood next to Kiser who smiled up at me. "We had fun. He learned about the babies. After we left the hospital, we went to Jaxson's."

"Good. Kiser, hang with your uncle while I walk Delilah out." Kellon handed the bag to Khiver and grabbed my hand.

While we rode the elevator down to the lobby, I eyed my man with amazement. Seeing him in his element in the studio turned me on beyond belief. Nothing felt better than watching your man not only work but dominate in his purpose.

Leaning against my car, I waited for him to speak. He hadn't said anything to me since we walked out of the studio. Part of me was on edge thinking he was about to give me another mouth full about him being disappointed in me for going to Jamaica.

When his hand raised, and those fingers started moving, I melted. He grinned, flashing me with that panty dropper smile. Using sign language, he asked me about my day. I opened my mouth to respond, but he shook his head. I signed back and told him that I had a good day.

Leaning down, he kissed me. Swooning uncontrollably, I watched him sign to ask me out on a date tomorrow. Just us. Blushing, I nodded and signed back asking what time I needed to be ready. He told me he'd let me know after he tucked me in tonight.

The icing on the cake, he signed that he loved me. Unable to contain my desire any longer, I jumped in his arms and devoured his sexy face with kisses.

KELLON

My morning started out the same. Standing by the window watching Delilah sleep and thanking God for another day. I planned an entire day for just her and I. As much as I wanted Kiser to come along, he had to sit this day out. My house was out of order, and I needed to get it back in alignment. If my house was out of sorts, then I knew Kiser would feel it. Delilah unknowingly demanded my attention and I planned on giving it.

A soft knock came from the door before Kiser peeked his head in. I made a mental note to talk to him about that. Most mornings I awoke Delilah up in ways that no child should be subjected to being traumatized in seeing at such a young age. I warned him about my mannish flirting but seeing us in the full act couldn't happen. Had he come in five minutes from now, his view of Mrs. Delilah would've changed.

"Dad, what time do I need to get ready?" Kiser asked as he tiptoed over to where I stood.

Him calling me Dad took me by surprise. I hadn't expected him to call me that for some time. Until he felt I deserved the title. Until he trusted me more.

Running a hand over my head, I sat down on the chair across from the bed. "Um, you got some time, little man. Why you up so early?" I shifted my attention back to a sleeping Delilah. She was awake. Her eyes were still closed, but her breathing had changed.

"I get up early all the time. I think better when I'm up early. Oh, I forgot to give Delilah her gift. I'll be back." Kiser tiptoed back out the room.

Making sure he closed the door, I looked back at Delilah. She now sat sitting up against the headboard watching me.

"Finally got to hear someone other than me call you daddy. How does it feel?" She gave me a small smile. The sadness was still evident in her eyes. It dimmed every day. Her meeting Kiser helped the light come back.

"Feels different than I expected." I cleared my throat to clear the emotions. "Thought he would wait a minute. Honestly, I prepared to never hear it." I shrugged.

The bedroom door flew open as Kiser came bouncing back in with a medium sized gift box in his hand. Climbing up the bed, he placed the box in Delilah's lap and sat next to her. "This is for you, Delilah. I told my Mom that I wanted to give you a gift."

"Aww, thank you, sweetie." She kissed his cheek. Unwrapping the wrapping paper, she pulled out a model car painted in hot pink and yellow with Baby Whisperer spray painted on the side. "This is so cute. I love it. Thank you." She grabbed him into a hug and sprayed his face with kisses.

Scooting closer and getting under the covers with her, he took the car out the box and began explaining the history of the old car. Moving quietly to the other side of the room, I grabbed my phone and snapped pictures of them together.

My family.

Taking a chance, I posted the picture on my IG page and decided to let the pieces fall where they may.

"Hey, Dad, can you teach me sign language too? I want to be able to talk with Mrs. Delilah when she isn't wearing her hearing aid."

I watched Delilah's bottom lip poke out and tremble. She was such a crybaby. "Yeah, I can teach you, or she can." I winked at her as she wiped her face.

"I can't wait to learn. Maybe we can come up with our own secret code like on Black Ops."

Delilah giggled. "That would be cool. I'll help you."

Feeling left out, I made my way towards the bed and got in behind Delilah. "Kiser, I'm taking Mrs. Delilah out for the day. You cool with hanging with Khiver?"

His eyes widened in excitement. "Yeah, that's cool. I like Uncle Khiver. Dad, can I ask you a question?" I nodded my head kissing on Delilah's shoulder trying to cop a feel on the sly. "Can we go to the Daytona 500? It's in Daytona. It's three and a half hours if we take I-95."

"That sounds fun. Yeah, Daddy, can we go?" Delilah pushed her butt against my hard dick.

"We can go."

"Yes. I'm going to call my Mom." He hopped off the bed and ran to his room.

The door hadn't closed all the way before I had Delilah over my shoulder headed to the bathroom. "Kellon, put me down." She giggled.

"No, ma'am. You about to convince me why I agreed to stand out in the damn Florida heat at a boring ass race show."

DELILAH

"**D**elilah, woman, if you don't get that stank ass fish from my face," Kellon threatened me. With each step I took closer to him the more he tried to hide behind X.

"Babe, it's a fish. What harm can it do to you?" I wiggled my brows causing him to frown. "Take a picture with me pleeeaaasseeee." I poked out my bottom lip and batted my eyes.

"People thought Jaws was just a cute fish. Can't believe you got me doing this lame shit." Grumbling, he stood next to me but not too close to where the large exotic fish could touch him.

"Alright now happy couple. Say cheese," Diego said as he took the picture. "Aww, boss, you look adorable." He teased causing the others in our group to laugh.

"Diego, you gon' end up swimming with Shamu over there." Kellon waved him off and moved out of my way so I could place the fish back in the tank.

When Kellon said he had an entire day planned for me, the last place I thought we would end up was the Miami Seaquarium. The place where he took me for our first date. My love for the aquatic life explained the dozen or so fish tanks in our home.

Kiser said he was okay with hanging with Khiver for the day, but I missed our little man. I wanted him to share this moment with me. With us. It felt like someone was missing, and that was him. In the short amount of time that he has been with us, he has become a part of our family. Kellon reassured me that we would have more moments to bring him along, but we needed this day for ourselves.

With his hand tucked away in the back pocket of my jean shorts, he kissed along my neck not caring that we were amongst other people. "What's on your mind, Mama?" Kellon asked as we followed behind the tour guide.

"Are you happy, Kellon? You always ask me, but what about you?" I kept my attention on the tour guide to avoid seeing his reaction.

I got a call from my mother-in-law this morning that opened my eyes to things I hadn't paid attention to. My in-laws were second parents to me. They loved me and cared for me far greater than I could ask for. Though the conversation was brief, less than five minutes, she made her point by the time we said goodbye.

Are you taking care of home, Delilah? The same way Kellon is there for you, are you there for him? Are you a helpmeet or a pain in the ass? By the time she finished grilling me, I stood in the middle of the bedroom floor pissed off that not only did she just check me, but I slipped up on my duties as a wife.

It seems like once we got off tour, all hell broke loose and neither of us, well me, had done anything to steer us in the right direction. I kept saying that Kiser being here didn't bother me. In truth, it didn't. Once I laid eyes on the smaller version of my husband I fell in love with him as if he were my own.

Part of me used the situation to my advantage and milked Kellon's need to kiss my ass for his screw up. All of that was fine and dandy until I openly said I accepted the child. After I said those words, it was time for me to move on. However, I did the total opposite. I ran and threw myself one hell of a pity party. Whoa, it's me, read bold on the banner.

So, when my mother-in-law checked me, I realized that I haven't checked in with my other half. Asked how he felt. Asked about his new journey of fatherhood. Asked what I could do to ease his mind. Yeah, I'm selfish. I own that.

"Aye, stop walking." He grabbed my hand and stared down at me with confusion. Those thick dark eyebrows slanted into a frown. He searched the depths of my eyes until he found what he was looking for. "Diego, pull up the truck. Anything else you want to see before we go?"

Dropping my head, I answered. "No, but…"

"Alright let's go." With one last glance, he looked at me intently, then strode towards the front entrance following behind X. The only time he stopped marching was if a kid asked for a picture but other than that he had tunnel vision for the exit.

I kicked myself for asking him that question in the setting we were in. Kellon had no problem answering me, the problem was the fact that we were out in public, and anyone could overhear our conversation. The stories that the media posted about him were all fabricated. He never put his business out there for anyone to have anything to say.

"Kel…"

"What makes me happy, Lilah?"

We were sitting in the back of the truck driving around Miami with no destination in mind. The customized truck had the seats set up with them facing each other. Usually, he and I sat next to one another. Not this time. He wanted us face to face.

"That's not what I asked, Kellon." I gave a small smile.

Running a hand over his waves he chuckled. "Mama, you can answer…"

"Dammit, Kellon. I asked a simple question that requires a simple answer." I squeezed my eyes and sighed. "I'm sorry. That wasn't called for. I…"

"What you want me to say, Delilah? Huh?" He moved down to the edge of the seat with his elbows resting on his knees. Those thick eyebrows were knitted together, and his nose flared. "Want me to say that you're selfish as hell? Or that you can be self-centered sometimes? That's what you want me to say? Fine. Delilah, I am happy with you, but you are selfish when it comes to how you move, Mama. You don't think about how your actions will affect anyone else but you."

I willed myself to cry. Squeezed my eyes until white specs covered my vision. The only thing that filled with tears was my heart. It constricted until a sharp pain shot through it. My emotional reactions to us lately had been bipolar. One minute you couldn't get me to stop crying and others, well most days, I sat emotionless.

"March 7th, September 14th, May 22nd." My lips trembled as he spoke each date out loud. "I watched you jump for joy. Cry tears of excitement. I watched you rearrange the plans we set up for our future to include a child. Then, I watched you cry tears of pain. Cry tears of loss. Watched you sink into depression. Questioned your worth. Question God. Then, I watched you repeat the same cycle two more times." He leaned back into the seat and sighed.

"I wiped every tear. Encouraged you to see that you weren't inade-quate as a woman. Prayed endlessly over you. Held your hand through it all. Questioned my own faith and wondered why God made you suffer for my sins. Seeing the woman you love fall apart, I felt like I wasn't doing my part as a man because I couldn't make you smile.

Here I am worrying about if you ate or not while I'm silently hurting because whether you realize it or not, those kids were part of me. *We* went half on a baby. My feelings were shoved to the side because the only person who mattered at that moment was you. I get it. It was your body. You carried them. But I was their Father too!" He yelled causing me to jump.

What happened to me not being able to cry? Want to put me in my feelings? Place my husband in front of me. Let him be disappointed in me or tell me that I hurt his feelings. All Kellon had to do was yell at me, and I became a bag of water.

Scooping me up in his arms the best way he could maneuver in the back of the truck, he placed me on his lap and held me like a baby. "Chill, man. You are defeating the purpose of me yelling." He chuckled while I cried harder.

"Ima tell Bishop if you divorce me. He gon' shoot you." I said between my hiccups. My gaze clouded with tears as the realization of the 'D' word might become a possibility if I stayed stuck in my ways. "Y-You can't divorce me, Kellon. We said un-until death do we part." I babbled on like a crying fool.

Placing a finger to my lips, he shushed me. Squeezing me closer to his chest, he looked down at me as if he were photographing me with his eyes. The tingle in my stomach grew with each blink. The very air around us seemed electrified by the minute.

"Delilah Mari, I couldn't divorce you if I somebody paid me to. When I married you, I married your flaws. Married the changes that would occur as we grow older. I knew you were selfish when you wouldn't let me cheat off your test in class." His smiled deepened into laughter.

My hand moved on its own accord from his cheek to his jawline. "Forgive me for only thinking of myself. I feel horrible not considering your feelings. I'm such a horrible person. A horrible wife." I hid my face in the crook of his neck.

"Look at me, Mama." He said in a low, composed voice. Shifting in his arms, I moved until I came face to face with those coal orbs. "I married you because I knew life wouldn't make sense without you. The man that I have changed into can deal with your spirit of selfishness. Going forward, I need you to remember that when you said I do it stopped being about you and it became you and me. In our union, we vowed to ride the highs and lows together. Remember that, okay?"

Looking up into the eyes of the man I vowed to spend forever with, my heart lurched madly. Running a hand over his smooth onyx waves, I loved him with my eyes. My heart fluttered wildly in my chest. "Will you marry me?"

He threw back his head and let out a great roar of laughter. "Yes, I'll remarry you every day of the week. Now open that mouth and kiss me."

There isn't a woman alive who is madly in love with the man of her dreams that can tell me she doesn't find joy in putting on that little black dress, the high heeled stilettos, lace lingerie to make the Pope blush, spraying on a fragrance that will bring him to his knees, and lipstick that sends his mind back to the night you made him scream until his toes curled.

The last outing on our day date ended at Rose. The lounge sat decked off in the hood with an ambiance that outshined any upscale restaurant. What I loved most was the live band that played old school music and featured some of the best jazz players in the south.

Justine and Harold Greene, the owners, served the best soul food I ever tasted. Drinks were worth the drive and the customer service perceived our expectations each time we ventured back into Kellon's old neck of the woods.

My cheeks hurt. Stomach cramped. And my heart felt more alive than it had been in months. The source of this new happiness? Kellon 'KC' Cambridge. Damn, this man rocked my world.

Dressed in a black suit with an olive-green button up that he left the first three buttons open on, I had the honor of being his date. As much as I drooled over the rapper who wore sweats on most days and jeans on the others, it all came full circle when he put his grown man on and stepped out in a suit. Kellon became the uterus shifter because that's what ended up happening after I took his jewels in the back seat of the car.

"Tell me more about wanting to be a midwife?" We sat in the back of the lounge in the corner with the perfect view of the band. He sat next to me with his hand resting on my thigh.

"Well, while Woody and I were in Jamaica, I did a lot of soul-searching. The pain I felt had to be turned into sunshine. After much prayer and meditation, I realized that me not being able to have children at this moment or ever was bigger than me. Bigger than us. Kiser is our newborn baby in a sense. We are learning what it means to be parents. To be honest, it seems kinda unfair for me to want us to try to have a baby to compensate for a void when we have him.

The pain I endured by losing those babies caused my heart to open more. My knowledge expanded. My wisdom has surpassed those who I seek for counsel. I'm able to direct that pain and suffering into positive energy used to help other mothers. That's my calling. Help woman who have suffered through miscarriages and help moms have a safe delivery." If I could pat myself on the back, I would. My own growth and maturity surprised me.

Kellon brushed a gentle kiss across my forehead. My calm was shattered by the hunger of his kisses. The cruel bliss of his mouth tantalized me. Fed me. "I'm proud of you. I admire your strength. We can wait to try again, but that doesn't mean we can't practice." Between each word, he planted kisses on my shoulders, neck, and face.

Drinking in the sweetness of his kiss, I separated our lips. "Thank you for supporting me. Are you excited about the new label and clothing line dropping? Kiser and I can be your personal models."

"I'm glad you mentioned that. Besides dropping a single here and there I'm going to place my album to the side right now."

My heart dropped. "Babe, why? I don't understand."

Grabbing my head between his hands, he forced my lips open with his thrusting tongue. Had me wishing that it was something else thrusting between my other set of lips. Realizing what he was doing, I snapped out the mastery of his kiss and scowled at him. "Stop, Kellon," I whined in between giggles. "Answer me. Is this because of the way I was acting?"

Pressing one last kiss to the top of my head, he leaned back and pulled me closer to his side. "Partial reason. But nah, these last few months we've gone through some shit, and it has opened my eyes to see that I need to be here. I'm taking the rest of the year off and devoting my time to my family. You've dedicated so many years and sacrificed so much for me that it's only right I do the same as you start this new adventure. I want to help you get your business off the ground.

I ain't delivering no babies or no shit like that, but I know what it takes to run a successful business. Plus, I want to spend time with Kiser. It's all about balance, and that's what I'm doing."

Why was he perfect? The perfect man for me. Downing the rest of my drink, I picked up a napkin and dabbed my neck. "Can we go home now? You got me feeling all hot and bothered talking like that."

KELLON

"It's hot as shit out here," Khiver groaned, expressing what the rest of us were feeling. I loved my son. Loved him dearly. Would lay down my life for him and take a bullet. However, never in my life will I ever agree to spend the weekend in Daytona at the Daytona 500 in this hot ass heat.

"I need to stop hanging around y'all heathens. Only reason I'm suffering in this heat is because I'm around a bunch of hoes." Pops grunted.

Glancing over at Kiser and his brothers smiling and laughing, it made the heat rays less scorching. Delilah convinced me to extend the invite to Sasha and her family. Kiser missed his brothers. The summer was slowly coming to an end, and I knew he would appreciate hanging with them more than us.

The boys took pictures, sat in the race cars with the drivers, and Kiser even drove one of the cars with the help of a racer. I thought the cameras and crowds would overwhelm him. Kiser sucked up all the attention and used it to his advantage.

"Will, you doing alright over there?" My Mother asked Will who sat under the shaded tent. He looked better than the last time I saw him.

Sasha hugged Delilah and I both when they arrived yesterday, thanking us for the new doctors who helped him recover.

"Yes, Mrs. Cambridge. I got all my energy. Can't miss KC perform."

I blamed Kiser for making me perform at this hot ass stadium. After being introduced to a few sponsors and the big wigs, he asked them why they didn't ask his dad to perform. All of a sudden, the wheels got turning, and an offer was made. Khiver called up DJ Skew, and here we were fifteen minutes away from hitting the stage.

"Mama, come here." Both Delilah and my Mother stood. "Really, Ma?"

"Hell, be more specific on who you are calling." My Mother kissed my cheek before walking back over to where my Pops sat.

"Hey, baby. You ready?" Propping her chin in the middle of my chest, Delilah wrapped her arms around my waist.

"I am. Don't let these snow bunnies out scream you." I reached up behind her ear and turned the hearing aid off. She flinched and dropped her eyes when I asked what was wrong. I knew I hadn't seen things. Delilah hadn't been wearing her hearing aid more often than usual. She even favored her right side when it came to laying her head down.

Sensing my worry, she changed the subject and kissed me. "I love you. Have fun up there." She backed up and moved over to where Kiser waited. They were going to stand on the platform in front of the bleachers while I performed.

"KC, it's show time, baby." DJ Skew called out to me from the stage.

Against my better judgment, I shrugged off Delilah's discomfort and mentally tapped into my music creativity realm. "Daytona, how y'all doing?" I yelled into the mic.

Since I started rapping, my fan base has always been diverse. My music drew people from all walks of life. Standing up here on the stage hearing the screams and cheers gave me much pride, but most of all, I felt blessed to perform in front of my family. My parents have always been cool with whatever decision Khiver and I made as far as our careers. Being that my Father was in the streets and we were by his side, all he asked was that we didn't stay. Make our money and leave. We did that.

"Kiser, where you at, man? I thought we were going to do this together?" Kiser's eyes ballooned, and his mouth dropped. Chuckling, I instructed Diego to bring him to me. "Bring your brothers with you." Once they were on the stage, DJ Skew dropped the beat making the crowd go crazy.

My chest swelled with pride watching my son rap alongside me. He knew word for word. Even his little brothers knew my lyrics. At one point I gave him the mic and let him rock the crowd. Delilah stood next to my parents smiling and rapping along too. By the time I finished my set, the crowd had tripled, and Kiser felt like he was the celebrity. He could have it.

My attention drifted back to Delilah. She wasn't in the same spot I left her in. When I asked Khiver where she was, he informed me that my parents took her back to the hotel. She started to complain of a headache and that her ears were bothering her. I knew it was deeper than that.

"Awesome show." Sasha smiled as I walked the twins over to her.

"The crowd went crazy. I don't know how you do it." Will stood and dapped me up.

"Thanks. I appreciate it. Ki, you rolling with me or your mom?" I needed to go check on my wife. Something told me that her headaches were more severe than what she was telling us.

"Um, can I stay with you?" Kiser gave his mother a somber look. I knew he wanted to go with me, but he also didn't want to hurt her feelings.

"You sure you don't want to spend time with your brothers?" Both twins had latched onto him the minute they reunited. Part of me felt sorry for keeping them apart. Sooner or later they would have to get used to the idea that their big brother had another family outside of them.

Kiser glanced over his shoulder and looked at his brothers. "I do. Will you come get me later? Please?" I thought I softened up because of Delilah. With Kiser, I became borderline weak and allowed him to have whatever he wanted. The relationship that he and I developed reminded me so much of the bond my Father and I shared. In just a summer, Kiser and I bonded far more in-depth than I imagined.

"How about you join us for lunch? Will is heading back to the hotel to rest, and we can take the boys to get something to eat?" Sasha was two seconds away from me sticking my foot upside her ass. I regretted inviting her to come this weekend. My innocent jester had somehow given her the impression that that meant I was checking for her or it was okay to be up in my space like my wife or her husband weren't sitting right there.

"How about no. Kiser, call me when you're ready to be picked up. Either me or Uncle Khiver will come get you. If not, I'll see you at dinner." Refraining from Kiser witnessing me cursing his mother out I walked off.

***

"I don't appreciate this secret lover's convo y'all got going on like we not sitting here." Smirking, my mother playfully bumped her hip against Delilah's.

For the last few hours Delilah had only been communicating through sign language. I knew how much she preferred to see me sign versus when I spoke. Most of my family were fluent in sign language. Just as I took an interest in it to learn so I could communicate with Delilah on all levels they did the same.

When I got back to the hotel, Delilah was laying in the middle of our bed balled up with an ice pack over her ear. My mother told me that on the way up to the room, she became lightheaded and just so happened a doctor was riding up with them. After checking her out, he determined that she was dehydrated from being out in the heat all day, and the headaches came from the fluids backed up in her ear.

A simple ear infection wasn't so simple for my baby. Most of the time it caused her to stay in the hospital for days until the swelling and fluid backup lessened. This ear infection had been going on for over a week now and not once did she mention anything about being in pain. I tried to keep my mouth shut and not go off because I knew that wouldn't change anything.

"She can't hear you, Ma." Standing, I walked over to Delilah and tugged her into my arms. "What did the doctors say?" Taking advantage of the backless blouse she wore, I rubbed the bare skin of her back and shoulders. I wanted to hear my favorite sound. Lowly, only for my ears to hear, she purred.

Oblivious to our secret lovers fondling, my Mother sighed heavily as she walked into the kitchen and grabbed one of the ice packs from the freezer. "There is nothing they can do until she gets home. Here, this will help with the swelling." Tapping Delilah on the shoulder, she showed her the ice pack and motioned for her to lean her head on my chest.

On first contact, Delilah flinched from the cold compress. "Keep it on there for about ten minutes. Whenever you guys are ready to go to dinner let me know."

I waited until my mother left out our suite before I picked Delilah up and carried her to the couch. Placing her on my lap, I studied the swollen left side of her face. In a matter of four hours, her left ear had turned red and swelled to the point of pain. The fluids in her ear caused her eardrums and outer ear to swell.

"Can you hear me?" I asked lowly into her right ear.

Nodding with reassuring eyes, she answered me. "Yes."

"Explain to me why you didn't tell me about the infection, Mama. This trip could've waited until you were better. Kiser would've had to watch it from the house." It pissed me off that she hid her pain from me. Her trying to put on a façade that she was okay to please Kiser only made it worse. The Daytona 500 happened every year. We could've brought him next year.

"At first, I thought I'd be better by the time we left to come here. Dr. Nathan said my hearing test came back showing I was losing more and more of my hearing. Then the infection came out of nowhere. All I wanted to do was spend this weekend with our family and deal with the reality of the situation when we got back," she spoke as her eyes bordered with tears.

Taking deep breaths to refrain from yelling, I spoke calmly. "Lilah, I get that, but you still haven't answered my question. Why didn't you tell me? Was I the only one present when we agreed to communicate no matter what?"

Dropping her head, she answered me in a soft tone. "I'm sorry,

Kellon. This weekend was about Kiser, not me and broken ears. I wasn't trying to keep it from you."

We sat in silence for a few minutes. I tried to understand her reasoning to hide her discomfort and infection from me. My mind instantly drifted back to her in Jamaica. I had yet to understand her logic for fleeing. Keeping things from one another had never been our memo. We shared everything. I knew more about her monthly woman issues than her doctor. What had changed in our relationships for secrets to be kept?

"So, your left ear, the hearing is gone like one hundred percent?" To even speak that out loud angered me. I know she was incapable of controlling what was internally going on but placing herself in more discomfort to please a child made absolutely no sense whatsoever. Her health was on the line, and all she wanted to do was satisfy Kiser.

Instead of nodding, she signed yes. The pressure from the fluid build caused her head to hurt when moved. "Just about. I can't hear nothing out of that ear from the buildup of fluid, but I'm sure once Dr. Nathan flushes it…"

Her shoulders shook as she broke down in my arms. "Baby, don't cry."

Burying her face in my chest she cried harder. "What if I never hear your voice again? Or Kiser's?"

Lifting her head by her chin, I gave her words of encouragement. "Nah, we think happy, positive thoughts around here, Mama. That won't happen. I mean, did you forget that I'm better at sign language than you?" I kissed her button nose.

In the middle of her giggling, her stomach growled. "Can we go eat now?" Mention food and her entire mood went from death to skittles and rainbows.

"We can stay here and order room service."

"No, I wanna go out."

I called Diego and X and told them that we were ready to head out. Since it was our last night in Daytona, we all agreed to take the kids out to eat before we parted ways. Sasha and her slick behavior had me ready to cancel it and take my family back home, Kiser included. With Delilah not feeling well and the way my mood had shifted, I had no patience to deal with her bullshit if she tried anything.

One of the sponsors from NASCAR invited us to check out his new restaurant not far from the stadium. He ensured that security would be densely placed around the establishment. Not only were we dining here, but so were a few of the other race car drivers.

"Kellon, school starts in a few weeks. When are you bringing Kiser home?" Throughout most of the evening Sasha paid more attention to Lilah and me than her own family. I knew it wouldn't be long before her yap opened.

The private room worked out in my favor. It kept nosey people from staring at us and kept Sasha's stupid questions from being overheard. Discussing personal business in public, especially about my child, was off limits, and she knew that. I have never been one to hold private conversations in public.

All of us were seated at the large round dining table. Delilah sat on my right with Kiser on my left. Like any other day, I had her tucked against my side. I expected her to object when I said we could share the same meal. Instead of fighting me on it, she clung to my side and let me feed her as I did if we were in the comfort of our home. No one questioned it outside of Sasha who made it be known she wasn't a fan of our actions from the frown she wore.

At the mention of separating from Kiser, I became nauseated. I knew the day would come when he had to go back home but I wasn't ready, and apparently, he wasn't either from his outburst. "I don't want to go back to Dallas." Grabbing my arm, he continued to plead with Sasha. "Mom, I can come to visit on the weekends or when I have breaks. Please, can I stay with my dad?"

Instead of focusing her attention on Kiser, Sasha glared at Delilah. Catching on to me sitting up in my seat and scooting my chair back, my parents excused themselves and the kids out the room. "Who wants ice cream?" My mother asked them as one side of the table glared at the other.

When they walked out, it left me, Delilah, Sasha, Will, and Khiver. I know he stayed back to make sure I kept my cool and my hands to myself. My palms itched to strangle her until she got some sense.

Feeling like she had the floor, Sasha lost her damn mind. "How dare you try to take my child from me?" She stood screaming with her attention on Delilah. Will tried to refrain her, but she kept yelling. "He is not your son. He is mine. Just because you can't have kids doesn't mean you can take my son. Our so–"

The hasty speed from me rushing to my feet caused my thighs to bump into the table. "Have you lost your damn mind?" I snapped.

Sasha flinched, dropping down into her seat. Will said nothing. He knew his wife crossed the line and I dared him to say something. "Kel–"

"Nah, who do you think you're talking to? I don't care if my wife insults your mother, what you will not do is be disrespectful." With my eyes watching her every move, I sat down. "Repeat that hot garbage you were just talking. Cause I'm trying to see if what I heard is what you actually said."

Blinking and shifting in her seat nervously, she spoke to the table instead of my face. "I-I..."

"Oh, you can't talk right now? Let me make this clear; Kiser has not once said anything to either of us about him wanting to live with me nor have I mentioned it to him. Everyone right here heard it first." Feeling Delilah rub her hand on my thigh I turned towards her. "You good, baby?" She nodded with her eyes on Sasha. Turning my attention back across the table, I continued on, "What you need to realize is that Will is your husband, not me. We share a child, and that is Kiser.

I have no problem with him living with me. You've had him for the last eight years, but that's neither here nor there. We both played a part in the ignorance that involved our responsibilities as parents. You are his mother, Sasha. I will never deny that or try to push Lilah to take your place, but what you do need to understand is that she is his step-mother. The same as Will is his step-father."

Scooting closer to the table I pointed my finger in her face. "You know how I roll, Sasha. The disrespectful shit doesn't fly. I promise on everything I love, the next time you feel like rubbing in our hardships I will make you regret ever meeting me. There are only two things I act a fool about, and that's my family and my money. I don't think you wanna go that route with me."

"I'm sorry." Sasha gave her half-ass apology. Delilah paid her no mind. She continued eating like she wasn't even there.

Will shook his head at his wife. I know he was embarrassed by her actions. His face said so. "Delilah and Kellon, I apologize for my wife's behavior." He cut his eyes at her before turning back towards us. "Before coming here this weekend, we discussed Kiser coming to live you. My health is still up in the air, and we have two energized boys who care nothing that their daddy is tired. It's not that we can't care for Kiser, but we think this is the perfect opportunity for you and him to develop a relationship really. Kiser caught us off guard with requesting to live with you before we even had a chance to talk with you guys."

Under the table, Delilah squeezed my hand. Behind the glass she drunk out of I saw the smile on her face. "Let us talk to Kiser. Make sure we are on the same page."

"Understood. Again, I apologize." Will motioned for Sasha to grab her things. "We'll see you folks in the morning."

The minute Will and Sasha walked out Khiver busted out laughing. Delilah joined in shortly after. "What the hell is so funny?" I asked because I didn't see anything that was funny.

"You, fool. Bruh, I just knew you were going to leap over that table and knock Sasha out. When she opened her mouth, I prayed for her downfall." Khiver laughed.

Waving him off, I asked Delilah how she felt about Kiser staying with us permanently. "What's on your mind, Mama?"

She stopped laughing long enough to lean in and kiss me. "You don't even have to ask. I want my baby to live with us."

Tossing several bills on the table, I stood. "Then it's set. Khi, get the lawyer on this. I don't trust Sasha for shit."

My feelings towards Sasha and her scandalous ways hadn't changed. Verbally she agreed to let Kiser live with me, but I wouldn't put it past her to have the boys in blue knocking on my door talking about I kidnapped my child. I had too much at stake for her to get in her feelings one day.

DELILAH

"If you don't open it, I will." Woody reached across the table for the envelope in my hand.

In my hand were the results of the AMCB exam, the American Midwifery Certification Board. Right after we came back from Daytona I jumped into studying and going to classes to catch me up on new practices and so forth. Kellon spared no expense nor was he waiting until I got my certificate to start bringing my midwifery business into a reality.

While we were in Dallas with Kiser, Khiver and his parents were secretly working to make sure my birthing center, Delilah's Whispers, would be finished. I questioned why Kellon wanted to spend a week in Dallas before the school year started. He gave me some answer along the lines of giving Sasha time to spend with Kiser.

It all made sense when we landed and was driven in the opposite direction of our home. The tears overflowed seeing all the moms I helped throughout the years standing on the porch of the center. Even some of the doctors I assisted were present and offered to send clients my way once I officially became certified.

"No, ma'am. I'm waiting to open it with my baby. Now tell me why your boobs look like two watermelons." Woody had to be out her mind to think I hadn't caught onto the pregnancy glow.

Reaching into her purse, she took out a piece of paper and slid it towards me. "Guess who is going to be a godmommy?" She spoke as her voice cracked from the heavy emotion.

"Yesss," I squealed, not caring of the attention I drew. "Hug me, heffa." Standing, we hugged each other in the middle of the restaurant. "I'm so happy for you."

"Thanks, babe." Dabbing her eyes with a napkin, Woody smiled. "That husband of mine swears me being pregnant means that he can abuse my lady parts whenever he can. I knew he would be excited but not like that." She and I shared a hearty laugh.

"Have you thought of a birthing plan yet?"

"Duh, must you ask?" Dramatically, she rolled her eyes. "I want a water birth. Can you handle that?"

Acting oblivious to what she was asking, I twirled a piece of my hair around my finger. "What do you mean can I handle that?"

Kissing her teeth, she rolled her eyes. "Lilah, you aren't slow so don't start now. Heffa, I want you to deliver my baby."

With a hand over my chest, my mouth dropped open. "Really?"

Shaking her head at my dramatics, she started giggling. "Yes, really. Why you sound surprised? You're the best, why would I go to anyone else?"

"I feel special. Aww, I get to deliver my little niece or nephew." Truthfully, I felt honored. Going to nursing school and becoming a professional baby rocker gave me no experience to the real deal, and the fact that she trusted me to deliver her baby spoke volumes to me.

"I want a boy, but I'll take a healthy baby.

"Well, I want you to have a girl. Kiser gives me the blues, but I need a little girl to dress up and go for pani and medi dates." I clapped my hands excitedly.

Woody's eyes said what her smile refused to say. Though she was happy to be pregnant, she felt hesitant in her approach to tell me. She was too reserved because she felt I'd feel a certain way, but I didn't. Genuinely, my heart soared for my best friend. Her happiness meant a great deal to me.

"How have you been holding up? Are you guys thinking about

different methods?" See what I mean? Trying to take the shine out of her pregnancy announcement.

"For right now our focus is on Kiser and making sure the birthing center is set to go. To be honest, I can't tell you the last time I thought about having a child. Having Kiser has somehow healed me and made me content with what I have. If it's meant to be, then I pray God allows me to carry full term. If not, I'm okay with that." This feeling... new feeling... of gratefulness hadn't come overnight. Getting to this space came from hours of prayer and taking each day one day at a time.

"Gosh, I wanna be like you when I grow up."

"Shut up, Woody."

"No seriously. You are a strong woman, Lilah. I admire you for answering to your calling even though it requires you to work hands-on with your pain. Can't say I know women who could do the same."

"Thank you. If it weren't for God and my small tribe, I wouldn't be this strong."

The death of my parents taught me that living for today meant more than living for tomorrow because tomorrow wasn't promised to anyone. I learned that grudges and holding onto negative emotions solved nothing but rather hinder you from experiencing some of God's greatest blessings. Living with my grandmother taught me the many layers of a woman's strength. Outliving both of her children, she took the bad of the situation and turned it into a blessing.

Most people would question the act of God for taking children before the parent, but not my grandmother. She felt blessed that God chose her to be their mother and love on them until it was their time to go home.

Woody taught me to live on the edge. Embrace my femininity. Take pride in my curves that my man loved. Taught me that being confident didn't mean I was a conceited or a snobby individual. It meant that I knew my worth and value.

Kellon, my heart and world, gave me a love that can't be described other than saying it's unrelenting, sometimes a complex love, but nevertheless, *our type of love*. A bonus, his family. Seven years after the death of my parents and a month after my grandmother joined them, God blessed me with another set of parents that loved me as their own and a brother who protected me.

So yeah, my tribe may have been small, but each trial and tribulation I endured I came out walking victoriously because of my tribe.

Woody and I stayed at the restaurant for another two hours going over everything she wanted to experience during her pregnancy. Instead of a gender reveal party, she wanted the godparents to be present with her when she and Carter found out the sex. I had to remind her to calm down and bask in the moment. The woman already had her checkbook out to book a venue for a baby shower that wouldn't happen for months from now.

Walking into the house, the first person I saw was Kiser who had a plate full of food headed upstairs. "Hey, love, you going to bed already?" The sun barely set an hour ago. During the weekend we allowed him to stay up however late he wanted to.

Balancing his plate in his hand, he hugged me and kissed my cheek. "Yeah, dad said he needs some attention from you and unless I want an early lesson on how babies are made I need to go to the other side of the house." He shrugged like what his Father said was normal. "Goodnight, Delilah."

What else could I do other than shake my head? "Wow. Uh, goodnight, sweet pea."

Making my way down to Kellon's man cave, I stopped outside the door to listen. If music played, that meant my vocals were about be exercised. Hearing the voices from the television, I sighed as I opened the door slowly. That same sigh turned into a gulp as my steps halted. There, on the black leather couch, Kellon sat ass naked with nothing but black socks on watching ESPN. My mouth watered taking in the soldier standing at attention between his legs.

"Hey, what are you doing down here?" In that instance, my whole being seemed to fill with waiting and wanting

"Ki went upstairs?" He peered at me through slanted slit eyes. Every time his gaze met mine, I found myself turning my head. My heart turned over in response to his intense gaze.

Remembering what Kiser said to me about Kellon wanting attention, a brief shiver of awareness engulfed me. "Yes." Carried away by my own response of lust, I failed to notice when the music cut on. *Oh shit.*

"Good." One word. He spoke one word, and my knees were ready to give out from under me. Turning the television off, he hit the button for the lights to change to a red fluorescent. "Come out them clothes." He sat back down stroking my favorite lover.

From across the room, I could feel the sexual enchantment that made him so self-confident. "I-I have something to share wi-with you." I handed him the envelope.

Without opening it, he sat it on the sofa next to him. "Congratulations, baby. Take off your clothes." He shifted down on the couch until his head rested on the back.

I was powerless to resist. Obeying, I underdressed under his watchful eye. I won't deny the sense of urgency that drove my hands to move without hesitation.

Looking over my nakedness, he seductively said, "Good girl, now come wet my beard."

KELLON

The image before me almost brought me to my knees. Laying in the middle of my bed laid my world and my heartbeat. Despite the life I once lived God saw fit to show me a little more favor and give me the desires of my heart.

A family.

A wife.

A son.

My parents were healthy and traveling the world celebrating their fortieth anniversary. Khiver and I were in preparation of launching of our clothing line, Redemption. In all, life was good.

Stretching his small arms, Kiser glanced over his shoulder. "Dad, why you like watching us sleep?"

"Watching you all sleep helps me start my day. Come downstairs with me so we won't wake Lilah." Bending down, I placed small feathered kisses against her lips before going downstairs.

"How you like your new school?" I cursed myself every month I paid tuition for that expensive ass private school. I wanted him to go to public school so that he could get exposed to all walks of life, but Delilah changed my mind when she mentioned the potential danger he'd face by being a kid of a celebrity.

"I like it. Teachers are cool, and I have a lot of friends. Can you sign me up for soccer?"

Scrunching up my face, I asked, "Soccer? Who the hell you know plays soccer?"

"What you got against soccer? My teacher said I could get a full ride scholarship for college."

Damn. Were we talking about college already? These next ten years needed to go by slow. "If that's what you want to do."

"Good morning, my loves." Delilah glided into the kitchen kissing both Kiser and me on the cheek.

With a mouthful of cereal, Kiser told her about his interest in sports. "Guess what? Dad said I could play soccer."

Mirroring his excitement, she smiled, "That's exciting. I draw the line at driving a soccer mom van, though. The truck stays." She winked before turning to me. "Oo, babe, we can get matching bedazzled jerseys with his number on them."

"Aye, chill. Matching jerseys is fine but ain't nothing bedazzled going on my body." Sweeping her up onto the counter, she and I watched Kiser drain his bowl of cereal. Somedays it felt so surreal seeing him here. Seeing the interaction between him and Delilah.

"I have to get dressed. Uncle Khi will be here shortly."

Wrapping my arms around her midriff, I tugged her down until I fit comfortably between her legs. "How you feel about today?"

We were finally going to see Dr. Nathan and find out the test results from her last hearing test. After we came back from Daytona, we went straight to the hospital. It took three whole days to drain both ears. Like suspected, the damage from the fluid buildup left scarring.

Settling into the comfort of my arms, she locked herself into my embrace. "I'm optimistic. You?"

"Same, but I need you to stay in tune with me, okay? When Khiver gets here, we can roll."

"Delilah, please sit down. All this pacing around is making me dizzy." I knew she was nervous to hear what the doctor had to say. Hell, so was I, but I wasn't digging a hole into the ground.

Standing on the balls of her heels, she touched her lips to mine. "Hush now."

"You looking mighty tasty in that skirt." Blushing, Lilah arched her neck and pecked my lips. Wanting more than the teasing kisses she gave, I slid my tongue into her mouth and took hold of her tongue. Sucking until she purred, I bit down on her bottom lip. Leaning back, I smirked and licked my lips. "Bend over so I can feel on you."

Trying to get out of my hold she whined, "Noooo. Okay fine, only the tip." One kiss to her covered nipples changed her mind.

Easing the lacy cup covering her mounds to the side I placed my face in the crook of her neck inhaling her scent. "Mmm, you smell good. Put your leg up here." My hands moved under her dress to skim her wide, thick hips and thighs. "Damn, and you got the nerve to be walking around with no panties. Turn that ass over."

Capturing a bud in my mouth, her nipples firmed instantly under my touch. "Oh my, Kellon, no." She giggled trying to push my head back.

Grabbing her hand, I placed it in my sweats and wrapped it around my swollen hardness. "Mama, give dad…"

"Am I interrupting?" Dr. Nathan smirked as he walked in catching us red handed.

Without turning around, I placed one last kiss on her nipples before covering her up. "Yeah, you actually are. Come back in fifteen minutes."

Smoothing down her dress, she pushed me aside. "Kellon, hush. Hi, Dr. Nathan."

Smirking, he greeted her, "Hey, Delilah. How are you feeling?"

"I'll know once you tell me the test results."

"Okay, no problem. Have a seat for me." Instead of listening she stood next to me biting on her bottom lip. "Your right ear has twenty percent, and the left has five. That ear infection nailed the nail in the coffin."

Before the reality of what he said sunk in, I placed her on my lap.

"What options do we have?"

"Implant surgery. We'll take a plastic silicone eardrum and recon-struct her ear. Pros are you can get seventy-five percent of your hearing back. Cons, you'll be prone to ear infections, but with the right medica-tion we can control the fluid buildup."

The thought of her going under the knife didn't sit well with me. "In the meantime, what can be done?"

"Same thing we're doing now. Draining the fluid as it comes. Unfor-tunately, I must advise that you are not to wear the left aid until it heals. You'll be dependent on your right side, and I'll prescribe you an antibi-otic for infections. Right now, it's pretty much a waiting game."

"Surgery sounds so..." she shivered. "Can we have time to think about this?"

"Absolutely. It's not like I can perform the surgery right now anyway. I could, but knowing your history, it will make you too high risk."

Her and I both looked at each other with confused expressions. "High risk?"

Dr. Nathan smile grew. "Yes. When I got the results back from your blood test, I wanted to shout for joy. Congratulations you two. How far along are you?" We said nothing. How could we when both of our jaws were laying on the floor? "Uh, are you not aware that you are pregnant, Delilah?"

A sob escaped her lips before she covered her mouth and shook her head. "Wow, um, I feel horrible. I'm sorry. Please forgive me for saying anything. I thought you knew."

Clearing my throat, I pulled her closer into me. She already sat on my lap, but I needed her as close as our bodies allowed. "It's fine. We had no idea."

Dr. Nathan looked genuinely sorry. He knew the hardships we faced when it came to conceiving. "How about I make it up to you? My Sonog-rapher is here today. Do you mind if she performs a sonogram?"

Delilah had no words. I answered for the both of us. "Sure. Thank you."

As soon as he walked out, she fell into my arms and cried. "Baby, everything is going to be okay," I repeated. My heart raced fast. Rocking her back and forth, I prayed and asked God to cover her and the baby. For her sanity and my own, I prayed he spared us from having another miscarriage. We couldn't take another one.

Shortly after Dr. Nathan walked out, a red-headed woman walked in pushing a machine with her. "Hello there, folks. My name is Olivia. Mommy, can you sit on the table and lie back for me?"

Olivia couldn't see Delilah shake her head. "Mama, look at me. Everything is going to be okay. Let the lady take a look, okay?"

Gripping her tighter in my arms, I stood and placed her on the table. When Olivia lifted her shirt both Lilah and I busted out laughing. Neither one of us questioned the little pudge she grew. Before the pregnancies, her appetite reflected my own. My baby could eat. We thought all those late-night runs to Krispy Kreme had caught up to her and explained the extra pounds she put on.

"Okay, this is going to be a little cold." Olivia squeezed a light blue gel on her stomach. "Oh my," She whispered.

"What's wrong?" Delilah sat up.

"Oh, nothing is wrong. The baby is quite big. See, take a look." She pointed towards the screen and there it was in black and white. "When was your last cycle?"

"Umm..." Her eyes widen. "Oh my gosh, Kellon, I haven't had a period in months. How did we not know?"

"That's perfectly fine. From the looks of things here, you're about fifteen weeks pregnant. Congratulations, mom and dad."

We stared at one another while she left. Caught up in our own shared moment of realizing that we were going to be parents. "Babe, we..."

"Hey now, none of that. We're pregnant, and from what she said we're already in the second trimester. You didn't make it this far with the others. We're going to make it, baby. You trust me?" I know it was wrong for me to sell her false hope, but this time felt different than the last. I had the confidence and faith to know that this baby would make it.

"I trust you."

"Good. We're going to be okay. The baby is going to be okay. I love you."

"I love you too."

DELILAH

"**B**reathe, Woody. Take deep breaths and exhale." Rubbing a hand across Woody's back, I coached her through the breathing techniques I taught her.

"Shit, D, it hurts," she whined as she swayed back and forth in the birthing pool. Her husband Carter sat behind her holding her hips and whispered soothing words in her ear.

"Come on, Woody. One more push." I leaned down and placed my hands under her body.

"Aye now, watch my baby," Kellon said from the corner of the room causing everyone to laugh. Keeping his word, he's been hands-on with the growth of my midwifery business. He usually stayed out the birthing rooms but being that it was Woody, he opted to be a part of the celebration and stayed in the corner.

"Kellon, shut up," Woody barked as another contraction hit.

"All I know is if she goes tipping over that pool, I'm spanking your baby right out the womb," he said pointing towards my seven-month belly. We all knew the plastic pool could do me no harm.

"Why must he be so stupid?" She laughed and cried at the same. "Arrgghhh."

My eyes widened in excitement seeing the head of hair come into view. "Here he is. Push, Woody." Three pushes later, and baby Carter August Jr. made his appearance weighing in at a whopping eight pounds and twelve ounces.

"Awe, Woody, he's adorable." I admired my godson over her shoulder.

Rubbing a hand over his back, she cried. "My precious baby boy."

"I love you, baby." Carter leaned down and kissed Woody.

"I love you too."

After making sure her overnight care was in place, I prepared to leave. "Woody, my work here is done. Donna and Karen will help you get cleaned up. I'll be back in the morning. Need anything before I go?" The two nurses on my staff were heaven sent, especially with me being this far in my pregnancy.

She shook her head with tears cascading down her face. "Thank you so much, Lilah. You truly are a blessing. I love you, boo."

"I love you too, babe. Get some rest."

"Congratulations. Take it easy." Kellon reached for my hand and purse.

Moments like today made the journey worth it. Since we opened our doors, I have delivered over twenty babies in the last four months. After finding out we were pregnant, I immediately feared getting out of bed. I placed myself on bedrest instead of listening to my doctor and family, who encouraged me to live life and enjoy the moment.

I quickly dusted off the negative thoughts when I got my first patient. The last thing I wanted to do was become a hypocrite to my patients, so I got out of bed and lived each day to the fullest.

We decorated the nursery, planned to have a gender reveal party, and I gave the duties of planning a baby shower over to Woody and my Mother-in-law. I thought positive thoughts and enjoyed my pregnancy.

I wasn't the only who enjoyed my round belly. Kellon and Kiser's hands stayed on my stomach. Kellon was worse. Even now he was driving with one hand on the steering wheel and the other moving clock-wise on my protruding belly.

"I'm surprised you stayed inside the room for the birth." Taking his free hand, I placed it on my lower abdomen so that he could feel the baby kicking.

"Where you are, so am I." Placing the truck in park at the red light, he leaned down and kissed my belly and then my lips. "Being hands-on covers everything, Mama. I'm not doing that for anyone else, but Woody is our people."

"I know. Did I tell you how much I appreciate and love you?"

Poking out his lip, he said, "No. You don't love me no mo'. If my name isn't Kiser or Kehlani, you don't pay me no mind." Leave it up to Kellon and Khiver to name my child Kehlani. Kellon said since I got to carry the baby it was only right that he picks her name.

After my giggle subsided enough for me to speak I asked, "Why must you lie? You know I have an undeniable love for my first big baby."

"We'll see when baby girl gets here. I'll ship her and her brother off to my parents if you stop giving me attention. Those titties were mine first. I already gotta share my bed with that wild sleeping little nigga, man. It's just screw me, huh? Pushing me out the way. Hell, I did all the work to create them." His mouth dipped into an even deeper frown.

"You mad. You big mad, huh?"

"I'm happy. Seriously, though, I'm grateful for it all."

"Me too. Ooo, give me your hand again." Every time the baby kicked I wanted him to feel it. We cherished these moments more than anything. With the first three pregnancies, we didn't get this far. Every day her kicks reminded me of God's promises and love.

EPILOGUE

K ellon

"H ey hey now. Don't get put in time out. Only your mama can make the stank face and get away with it." Kehlani's bottom lip poked out, and her face scrunched up in preparation for the scream she was about to release. "Aye, baby girl. I thought I was your favorite person? You gotta be quiet while your mama and big head brother sleep."

It happened. My morning routine changed. Watching Delilah sleep wasn't my only infatuation now. Kiser and Kehlani had been added to the mix. Both kids had their own rooms but somehow ended up in our bed by the time the sun rose.

"We got about ten more minutes before Mama wake up. You know she jealous that I'm your favorite. All she good for his popping out her titties and feeding both of us."

I couldn't get enough of staring at my baby girl. I stared at her in awe sometimes. We made it. She was real. Delilah carried two weeks passed her delivery date and endured eighteen hours of labor. How she did it, I never wanted to find out, but I thanked her daily for sacrificing her body to bring our daughter into the world. Woody and my Mother thought she lost her mind when she opted out of having an epidural. The entire time she was in labor she didn't crumble or give in. She sat in the birthing pool and pushed out Kehlani on her uncle Khiver's birthday.

"I heard that and stop talking to her like that. Bad enough Kiser is picking up on your habits." She stomped into the nursery with a frown on her face and her arms crossed.

"Who pissed in your cereal?" Delilah knew her temper tantrums were a turn on. If I weren't holding Kehlani, I'd readjust that attitude.

Punching me in the arm, she said, "You did that's who. Round here shooting up people's club like that mess is funny. She's only a month and a half old, Kellon." She stomped her feet whining.

Oblivious to what I did to piss her off I laughed, "Mama, what you are talking about?"

Shoving the pregnancy stick in my face, she gritted, "This is what I'm talking about, Kellon. Oh, my God, I can't believe this. Two babies in one year! Kellon, keep your hands off me." She threw the test at my head and stormed out of the room.

Glancing down, Kehlani was all smiles. "Shit, your Mama been married to me for almost ten years. What would possess her to think I'd wait six weeks for a Doctor to tell me when I can hunch my wife? Looks like you about to have another little brother. That's why you been giving your mama hell lately, huh?"

Almost two years from the date we suffered our last miscarriage I became a Father of two with one on the way. Staring down into the eyes of the creation my wife and I created, I couldn't help but become overwhelmed with emotion. God restored everything we lost. We had three kids after losing three.

I thought back on what all transpired after my last tour. If I hadn't resigned, who knew what shape my marriage would be in right now. Did I miss performing? Yes, but being with my family triumphed screaming fans.

Every day I got to experience the greatest joy by seeing my loved one's faces. Taking care of them. Providing for them. Delilah asked if she needed to sit out from working and I told her no. I looked forward to becoming a stay at home father and caring for our children while she helped give another family the same joy we experienced.

I felt complete. My family was perfect.

The End.

ABOUT CHELSEA MARIA

Chelsea Maria is rebirthing the idea of love for the millennial generation. Armed with a desire to define the union of faith and love, Chelsea Maria writes relatable stories that challenges society's warped view of love. With a clearly defined purpose, Chelsea puts her passion and talents to use for the betterment of the generation.

Tasked with changing the narrative, Chelsea gives it her all. With no abandon, she pens fervently the stories of her heart and the hearts of her readers. Using her God-given talent, she employs wit and artistry to plant seeds of conviction and force reflection of her readers. Every addition to her growing catalog is penned with the purpose to revive the faith in love.

Now, with an arsenal of love-inspiring chronicles she is claiming her spot in the world of fiction. Bringing a new wave to the industry and reshaping the twisted perceptions.

ALSO BY CHELSEA MARIA

For You I Will http://bit.ly/ForyouIwill

I Should've Chosen You http://bit.ly/IShouldveChosenYou

Say You'll Never Leave http://bit.ly/sayyoullneverleave

Say You'll Be My Baby http://bit.ly/SayHeBeMyBaby

I'll Be Good to You (Young & Reckless Book 1) http://bit.ly/IllBeGood2You

A Love So Soft (Young & Reckless Book 2) http://bit.ly/ALoveSoSoft

More Than A Crush http://bit.ly/MoreThanACrush

When The Night's Over http://bit.ly/WhenTheNightsOver

My Heart Is Your Secret http://bit.ly/MyHeartIsYourSecrets

Chasing Empty Hearts https://bit.ly/ChasingEmptyHearts

LOVE NOTE

Hey loves!

Thank you so much for reading Kellon and Delilah's story. Punches of love and pages of romance. Can't get any better than that. I truly enjoyed writing their story, and I hope you enjoyed reading about them. As always, I want to hear from you. If you can be so kind to leave a review on Amazon or Goodreads, I'd greatly appreciate it.

Stay tuned for more information on my next release by connecting with me on:

I'm always dropping teasers and first glances at my covers in my reading group. Be sure to join by clicking: https://bit.ly/LoveOnTheLowFB

Lastly, if you aren't on social media and prefer email, please subscribe to my mailing list: http://bit.ly/subscribecmaria

Never goodbye but see you next release.

XOXO,

Chelsea Maria